The

Singing

and Dancing

Daughters

of God

The

Singing

and Dancing

Daughters

of God

TIMOTHY SCHAFFERT

UNBRIDLED BOOKS

This is a work of fiction. Names, characters, places and incidents either are the product of the author's imagination or are used fictitiously, and any resemblance to actual persons, living or dead, business establishments, events, or locales is entirely coincidental.

Unbridled Books
Denver, Colorado

Library of Congress Cataloging-in-Publication Data

Schaffert, Timothy.
The singing and dancing daughters of God / Timothy Schaffert.
p. cm.
ISBN 1-932961-12-7 (alk. paper)
1. Divorced men—Fiction.   2. Single fathers—Fiction.   3. Country
musicians—Fiction.   I. Title.
PS3619.C325S56 2005
813'.6—dc22
2005015899

1   3   5   7   9   10   8   6   4   2

Book Design by SH • CV

First Printing

For

Rodney Rahl

and my parents,

Larry and Donita

ACKNOWLEDGMENTS

Thanks to Alice Tasman and Jean Naggar, and Greg Michalson and Fred Ramey, for their commitment to my work. Also thanks to those who have read this book in various stages or have otherwise contributed to its development: Judy Slater, Gerry Shapiro, Leslie Prisbell, Justin Wolta, Janet Lura, Maud Casey, and Ladette Randolph. A few of the characters in this novel first appeared, in a somewhat different guise, in a short story that was published in issue 11 of the literary journal *Press*.

PART ONE

1.

TO get through the afternoons that wound into early evenings, driving a school bus along long country roads and driveways, Hud kept slightly drunk. He sipped from an old brown root-beer bottle he'd filled with vodka. There'd been a few times in the past when he'd gotten too drunk, when he'd swerved too much to avoid a raccoon, and even once a sudden hawk swooping too low. He made himself sick to think how he'd once nearly driven the rickety bus in all its inflammability into an electrical pole. He knew what an ugly notoriety such an accident would bring him. *The whole world,* Hud thought, *likes to mourn together and hate together when it can.*

There was a man in town named Robbie Schrock, who, like some fairy-tale hag, had murdered his own two boys with rat-poisoned candied apples he'd dropped into their Halloween sacks. When the children died, Robbie Schrock cried on the TV news and blamed the neighbors, and the whole little town cried with him, shocked by the inhumanity of some people. Robbie Schrock eventually confessed, and shocked the town all over again. The state tried and sentenced him and gave him the chair.

Today was the afternoon of the execution, and some of the children on Hud's bus celebrated by dressing up in Halloween costumes, though it was only early September. One boy wore a bandanna and a pirate's eye patch pushed up on his forehead. Another boy wore an Indian headdress and a breastplate made of sticks and feathers. A little girl was a Belgian nun in a pale blue habit and a winged wimple folded from newspaper.

Hud, disturbed by what he thought to be morbid spectacle, took a last shot-back of vodka from the root-beer bottle. He looked in the rearview mirror to the two boys sitting behind him. Both were dressed up in churchy blue suits, their faces painted a pale gray.

"What are you supposed to be?" Hud asked.

"We're the murdered Schrock boys," they said, their voices in tired and rehearsed unison.

"You're the worst of them all," Hud mumbled. He felt compelled to write a song for Robbie Schrock, though he'd hardly known the man and, of course, did not condone his crime. Whistling, Hud drove with one hand, and with the other he wrote down key words to the song coming together in his head. He wrote "lonesome" and "divorce" and "weakly" in ink on the leg of his jeans.

He understood something of Robbie Schrock's circumstances. Hud's newly ex-wife, Tuesday, at times was full of vindictiveness. For a short while she had conspired to keep

Hud's daughter away from him, judging him a drunk and a misfit and unworthy of even the few decent things this worthless world offered him. Robbie Schrock, his babies taken away, probably in an ugly divorce, probably left with only an occasional weekend or an occasional holiday with his children, wanted the whole world to know what loss can really do to a person. Hud could sympathize.

Though he would never hurt his own eight-year-old, his adorable Nina, he had thought about stealing her away, about painting his car a different color and driving and driving until they found some suitable no-place. They'd wear fake glasses, and when they spoke to the people at the gas stations and grocery stores, they'd cover their mouths with handkerchiefs to disguise their voices. He'd change the part in his hair and go by the name of some other Paul Newman character—Luke, maybe. Maybe Butch. Nina could choose her own name, would probably choose "Jessie"; that was what she named all her dolls.

Whenever with Nina, and only with Nina, Hud felt calm and attentive, and he thought if she was his all the time, he'd be a better man. A few weeks before, Tuesday had let Hud have Nina for an afternoon in his apartment above the shoe repair shop on the town square. Hud and Nina went up on the flat roof and harvested the tomatoes he'd grown in pots. Afterward, after eating some, Nina lay back to nap, seeds on her cheeks, and asked him to sing a song about her. He sat so his shadow kept the vicious sun from her skin, and he plucked a tune from his guitar. He called it "Nina Is All I Need, Really," and as she drifted off, he sang about every aspect of her face, giving her nose, her pink lips, the red freckle on her neck, each its own separate piece of melody. *This could be why people have children in the first place,* he thought.

Hud and Tuesday had one other child, a seventeen-year-old boy named Gatling, a real retro hipster with a slick pompadour, cuffed jeans, and dice tattooed on his bicep. Or at least, that was how he looked when last they saw him. Since he'd vanished on the first hot day in May, they'd received only postcards; he was touring with a band called the Daughters of God, playing guitar and singing backup at revivals and fairs.

Gatling was the reason Hud and Tuesday had married so young, and he'd been a handful for years. Once last winter, practicing some new brand of discipline she had learned about at a seminar, Tuesday had locked Gatling out of the house for a few days for giving Nina a drink of his Windsor Canadian. "I knew she wouldn't like it," he'd said, and though it was only a tiny sip that had dribbled mostly down Nina's chin, it had been the last bit of badness Tuesday would allow. And that was when he had started spending so much time at the Lutheran church, hanging out with a group of Jesus freaks and driving into Omaha with them to hand out pamphlets in front of rock concerts.

Gatling had also taken to scarring and cutting himself, had even carved all nine letters of his ex-girlfriend's name across his chest in an act so romantically psychotic it had almost won him Charlotte back.

All Hud knew for sure was that so much had stopped seeming possible that afternoon in May when Gatling left.

Hud remembered driving into the driveway, only seconds after Gatling had gone off for good on his Vespa, some ice cubes in the grass not yet melted despite the day's uncommon heat.

After dropping off the last of his costumed passengers, Hud went home to sit alone and compose some lyrics. Robbie Schrock's life seemed perfectly lived for a country song. Country songs, to Hud, were chronicles of destitution, haunted by beaten-dead wives and abandoned children. The key to an authentic country song, he thought, was to tell the story of a life lived stupidly and give it pretty strains of remorse.

Hud wrote: "He had the cheap kind of heart that broke when you wound it too tight." Then he wrote: "He got all turned around on what was supposed to be wrong and what was supposed to be right." Hud had spent many of the summer's days, the days following the finalization of his divorce, at his kitchen table writing songs and drinking Mogen David red like it was soda pop.

Hud climbed out through his window and up to his roof. The town square was usually quiet at night, but people continued to celebrate the execution of Robbie Schrock. The costumed children strung toilet paper in the trees on the courthouse lawn and knocked on doors for handfuls of candy. There were costumed adults on their way to parties: a man in a cape and top hat and white gloves alongside a woman wearing only a long red magician's box, her head and arms and feet sticking out, a saw stuck through the middle. A woman dressed as a nurse in blue jacket and white stockings pushed a pram jingling with bottles of liquor.

Hud, not amused, began to sing one of his more mournful songs, about a girl stung to death by wasps. He strummed a purple guitar. People passed in the street, but no one stopped to listen. No one wept for the man in the song sad about the death of his girl. No one even offered a knowing, sympathetic nod.

My neighbors hate me, Hud thought. They all knew and loved his wife. Tuesday taught art at the grade school, taught the town's children how to make tongue-depressor marionettes and abstract paintings using slices of old potato. *And they hate me now,* Hud thought, *only because I'm without her.*

2 .

ΔΔΔΔΔΔΔΔ

AFTER his rooftop performance, Hud suddenly remembered he was supposed to help Tuesday's dad at the drive-in; they were showing a movie with bloodsuckers and prom queens to further celebrate this mock Halloween, and they expected a late-night crowd. The Rivoli Sky-Vue was one of only a handful of drive-ins in the state, and one of only a few in the nation that still showed classic drive-in movie fare. All the spaghetti Westerns and the dirty wet-bikini flicks and the souped-up back-road racing movies were part of a private collection owned by Hud's ex-father-in-law. He even had a few out-and-out pornos that they showed from time to time after midnight. The Rivoli made little money, but it was the town's only tourist attraction and had been featured in *People* magazine and *Film Comment*.

Though the movie had started, Hud stood at the front gate taking admission for Tuesday's dad, who they all called Red though his head of thick curls had turned gray years before.

Red had a longtime girlfriend, the Widow Bosanko, the town's librarian. Hud remembered, from when he had checked out Zane Grey Westerns as a kid, how she always wore a bracelet of wooden cherries that knocked together with a pleasant click.

Alone in the drive-in's entryway, Hud collected a few of the summer's last fireflies, trapping them in an olive jar to bring to Nina, who enjoyed bugs. He was interrupted when Junior, a boy Gatling's age, drove up. You wouldn't know from Junior's piercings up and down both ears and his black-eye that he was the zealot responsible for Gatling's religious conversion. Now that Gatling was off touring with the Daughters of God, Junior dated Charlotte, Gatling's pensive ex-girlfriend.

Hud had always had a harmless crush on Charlotte that had been helped along a few nights before when he had seen her selecting songs at the jukebox at the Steak and Black Coffee, an all-night diner on the highway, her tongue at her lips in concentration. She wore a tight t-shirt pulled over the top of a sundress. After selecting a few dollars' worth of old country ballads like "Crazy" and "Cold, Cold Heart," she sat down with Junior, who bowed his head in prayer over his New York strip and hash browns. But Charlotte didn't pray along, involved as she was in the music, her coffee cup held still just beneath her lips as Hank Williams sang about the robin's lost will to live.

"Looking awfully lonely there tonight," Hud said. He peered inside the car to where Junior sat alone.

"Well, I tell ya, old man," Junior said, handing Hud $5 and shrugging, winking, "I think I scare all the pretty little girls away."

Hud leaned in more, looking beneath the steering wheel. He reached in to push the button to pop the trunk. "Ah, come on, man . . ." Junior protested. "You can't . . ."

Hud walked to the back to open the trunk lid, where he found Charlotte curled up. "Some date," he told her, taking her hand to help her step out. She wore a slick red robe patterned with bluebirds sitting on the branches of spindly trees. Her fine hair was knotted up atop her head and stuck through with black lacquered chopsticks.

"We're broke," she said, leaning back against the car, fanning herself with a fragile paper fan that featured faceless geishas fanning themselves.

"I would've let you in anyway," Hud said. He tapped a knuckle against her cheek. "I still like you some." Hud just barely kept himself from giving Charlotte a short kiss, just on the cheek or the forehead, just something friendly and fatherly. "Here," he said, handing Charlotte a pair of pink plastic fangs he'd been giving out to the children.

"If you were smart you'd get back with Tuesday," Charlotte said, moving the fangs between her fingers, pretending they were doing the talking.

"I happen to know that," Hud said. Just last Fourth of July, Hud and Tuesday had had a momentary truce, a few nights of reunion that involved popping off fireworks in the front yard. When night fell, Hud lit the expensive ones, the ones with all the color and noise, but he didn't watch the sky; he couldn't take his eyes off Tuesday, who sat with Nina on her lap, holding a parasol above their heads to protect them from the burnt shrapnel that fell from the sky. The summer had been dangerously dry, and they all looked a little nervously to the leaves of the trees, which rattled as the hot pieces of the spent fireworks rained through the branches.

Junior called out, "Lottie," a name Hud thought only he and his son called Charlotte, and Charlotte slipped away. As Hud walked to the side of the car, he saw Charlotte taking a drag off Junior's cigarette, the pink teeth loose in her mouth.

Hud became desperate to see his daughter, as he thought ahead, of her growing up only to become confused and lost and learning too much too fast. He hoped to God Nina never crawled into the trunk of a car at the request of a cheap boy.

Hud wanted to wake Nina up and pull her out of bed and rock her back to sleep. He wanted to count all her fingers and toes, and all the hairs on her head. He'd sneak in through the window, and he'd tell Nina, "Nobody else is worried about you. Just me. Everyone else sleeps through the night."

Hud drove quickly to the house and let himself in to find Tuesday sleeping on the sofa, the still hot coal of her cigarette burning a hole in the velveteen of the cushion. Hud sat on the coffee table and took the cigarette from her fingers. He leaned back, took a drag, examined Tuesday's costume—she wore a 1970s-style shirtdress, her hair swept up in a fresh beehive slightly crushed by the sofa pillow, a false eyelash dangling from one eyelid. A fake yellow bird with synthetic feathers sat perched in a small birdcage at the foot of the sofa. Hud couldn't figure out who she was supposed to be.

Tuesday had always slept the deadest sleep he'd ever witnessed—her body didn't move at all, not even with her breath. She usually stayed up late painting desert scenes on the skulls of cows and horses, then fell into her bed. Hud could too easily imagine all sorts of things happening in the night of Tuesday's deep sleep—a terrible storm, or a kidnapping, or a fire engulfing the entire house long before she choked awake on a single breath of smoke. *That's the only reason I drink,* he thought, crossing his legs, crossing his arms, blowing cigarette smoke toward Tuesday's face to test her as she slept. She didn't flinch. *I drink because I worry myself sick about my girls,* he thought.

He started to snuff the cigarette out in a glass ashtray, then recognized it as a souvenir from a family trip of years before. He picked it up and spat in it, then rubbed his thumb at the black. After rubbing some of the ash away, he could see the bare feet of Fred and Wilma Flintstone. Hud and Tuesday had taken the kids, with Nina practically just born, up to South Dakota one summer, where they had walked through Flintstone Village, taken a tour of a cave, and eaten in a cafeteria with a view of Mount Rushmore. Hud had bought Tuesday a locket of Black Hills gold that she had promptly lost when they went swimming in a naturally warm pool in Hot Springs. Tuesday had cried about it at the motel that night, upsetting Gatling a little, but Hud had loved it. He'd loved holding her and telling her they'd go back to the pool to search, or that he'd buy her another, cooing at her like she was a kid. He'd been glad she'd wanted the necklace so much because even back then, especially back then, they'd had many fights and troubles.

Hud got up and stuck the dirty ashtray in the saggy back pocket of his jeans as he walked through the kitchen, flicking the cigarette into the sink. A nightlight near Nina's bed lit the room enough for Hud to see Nina sleeping, still in a cowgirl costume, still even in boots and prairie skirt and Western shirt printed with yellow roses. A straw hat hung on the bedpost. Hud tugged on Nina's skirt, and she woke peacefully, too peacefully, Hud thought. "You shouldn't be sleeping next to an open window," he whispered, and Nina sat up in bed and puckered her lips for a kiss. Hud kissed her, then said, "Any creep could come along. Aren't you afraid of creeps?"

"Oh, sure," she said, shrugging her shoulders.

"Let's go for a drive someplace," Hud said. He opened the window and lifted the torn flap of the screen.

"OK," Nina said, standing up in the bed, "but first, don't you like my costume? We went to a party."

"It's nice," he said.

"I'm Opal Lowe," she said, and Hud was touched that she had dressed up like Opal Lowe, his favorite country singer. He'd taken Nina to a county fair a few weeks before to see Opal singing in the open-air auditorium. They'd had to sit far in the back on a bale of hay, had to strain to hear above the bleats and clucking of the animals judged in nearby pens, but Nina had loved it and had hummed along as Opal Lowe sang about her man's habits, how he liquored her up on Wild Turkey, lit her Old Golds, made her need him like water.

Nina said, "Can I bring my purse?" and she picked up a clear plastic purse from the end of the bed. Inside was a tube of lipstick, a little box, a comb, and a plastic baby doll's head with wild yellow hair.

"Sure, bring your purse," Hud said. He jotted a note in crayon: "I'll be back with her before sunlight, before you even read this," and left it atop the rumpled covers of the bed. Nina crawled onto his back, and they slipped through the torn window screen. He imagined never returning with her, imagined his picture next to hers on fliers sent through the mail.

"We'll go anywhere you want to go," Hud said, helping her into the car. "Should we go to some ocean far away? Go smoke a friendly cigarette with the fishies?" Nina laughed, and Hud said, "Go to Mexico for some cow-tongue soup?"

"No," Nina said. "Disgusting."

"We could go to Disneyland and ride a roller coaster," Hud said. "Just be careful not to spill your beer," and Nina laughed at the idea of having beer to spill.

Hud drove off toward the highway. "We could run away together for good," he said.

"I live with my mom, and you have to drive the school bus," Nina said, almost scolding.

"We'd write songs for a living," he said. "Our first song could be called 'Two Fugitives.' It'll go . . . um . . . 'We're fugitives from a bad life. Breaking free from . . .' From what . . . 'From the chains and shackles of separation and loss.'"

Nina sighed with disapproval. She'd become an expert fan of country music ever since Hud had taken her to see Opal Lowe. She turned on the radio now, as they drove to the edge of town, listening, hoping for an Opal Lowe. But instead they heard Chief Kentucky Straight, a man one-sixteenth Ogalalla

Sioux who sang of the pain of life on the reservation. They heard a choir of hard-living rednecks called the Widowmakers. Then there was Rose-Sharon and her Lilies of the Valley. Rose-Sharon was a woman with cancer who sang gospel. Nina sang along to her song called "I'm So Full of Jesus."

"What was your mom dressed up as?" Hud asked.

"A mermaid," Nina said.

"No," Hud said, but he thought a second, thinking of the bird, remembering Catherine Deneuve's canary in a cage at the beginning of *Mississippi Mermaid,* one of Tuesday's favorite movies they'd watched many times together. Deneuve hadn't had a beehive in that movie, he was almost certain, but rather a tall straw hat. He wondered if Tuesday had missed having him at her side at the party, someone who would truly appreciate the charm of her costume. He could have gone as her Jean-Paul Belmondo, but he would've preferred to be Belmondo in *Breathless* in fedora and sharp suit, puffing on a French cigarette.

It was Tuesday who had first called him Hud; when they were dating in high school, they stayed up late to watch the movie, just long enough for them both to be impressed by Newman's cantankerousness. "You've got his snarl and skinny legs," she said, then they nodded off to sleep long before Newman raped Patricia Neal.

Hud asked Nina, "Do you know why you even wore that costume today?"

"Well, you see," Nina said, "you see . . . there was this guy . . . and he was somebody's dad . . . and there were these boys . . . and the dad hurt the boys so bad that they were killed. And everybody dressed up because . . . um . . . there's going to be a funeral soon."

"Jesus," Hud said, sighing and shaking his head with frustration, "nobody even told you much about it, did they? They just let you get dressed up for their own perverted god-damn reasons."

Nina said, "I do so know everything about it." She looked out the car window. "And I hate it when you swear." She normally enjoyed when he let some swearing slip in front of her.

Hud took off down the unlit gravel roads, squinting into the dark, looking for the sign to tiny Rhyme, Nebraska. Behind a grocery store there lay an old Happy Chef, the thirty-foot-tall fiberglass statue that had once towered in front of a highway café. The store's owner had bought the statue long before, and it now rested flat on its back in the tall grass. Hud had brought Nina there last summer, and she had liked sitting in the Happy Chef's spoon.

Nina, not speaking to Hud, combed her long, white-blond hair. A strand flew in Hud's face, and he plucked it away and let it fly out the open window. They drove past a mailbox and a spooky crooked iron weather vane. Hud imagined Nina's strand of hair finding its way into an old house where a man lived alone, a man who had maybe killed his wife in silence and buried her in a small patch of his miles of untrespassed-upon land. Hud imagined the old man waking with the long hair on his pillow or finding it in his soup and from then on living in terror of what he'd done.

"What's the name of your doll there in your purse?" Hud asked, to get Nina talking again.

Nina looked down at her clear plastic purse and tapped her finger at the doll head inside. "It's not a doll," Nina said. "It's just a head. Heads don't have names," and she returned her stare back out the window.

Hud now felt entirely sober, and very tired. He wished he had just peeked in on Nina, had just watched her sleep undisturbed. *A good father,* Hud thought, *lets his children sleep through the night.* This was what Hud didn't like about being sober. He didn't like coming to his senses. Good sense can prevent a man from taking what he should have.

When Hud's car began to sputter, he stomped on the gas pedal, and the car went a little farther before sputtering again, then stopping. It wouldn't start back up. The needle of the gas gauge had been stuck on empty for years, and the odometer had read 138,323 for several hundred miles, but the old Pontiac and its habits had become so familiar to Hud over time that he'd thought he knew well how far he'd get on a full tank.

Before turning off onto the country roads, Hud had taken a deserted back highway, with no traffic across its broken pavement. They wouldn't make it back tonight on foot even if he could find the way. He tried to think of what else might be wrong with the car, something he could easily fix. He turned the key again and listened closely to the engine as it still refused to turn over. He became frightened, and he worried over all the destruction that was about to befall him. By not returning his daughter to that bed next to that wide-open window, in that house with the weak locks, where his wife slept through everything, everything for him could change.

He might be arrested. He might not be allowed to take Nina out again. He might lose his job.

"Goddamnit!" he practically screamed. "That bitch!" He pounded his fists against the steering wheel. He punched the horn at the center of the steering wheel, then drove his fists into it, holding the horn down to blare. The muscles in his arms were tight, and he thought if he pushed harder, he'd make the noise louder, deafening.

When he let up on the horn, the hollow silence of the night fell again, and he could hear Nina sobbing. Her face was turned away from him, and she held both her hands tight at her mouth, like she was trying to keep herself quiet. Hud gently pushed the hair from Nina's face and behind her ears. "Nina," he said, "I'm sorry. I should have just let you sleep." He should have just taken her out trick-or-treating, to collect some sweets and heave some bad eggs, like everybody else was doing.

"It's all right," Nina said, still crying.

Hud wiped her tears with his thumb. She swallowed hard, then wiped her face with her sleeve. She took from her purse a little hinged box and opened it. "I haven't shown you this," she said, her voice still all chokey. She displayed her collection of dead desert bugs, identifying each one—the brown recluse, the palo verde beetle, the tarantula hawk. When she touched her finger to a brittle scorpion's back, its hooked stinger broke off. When Tuesday and Hud first tried a trial separation almost a year ago, the fall before Gatling left, Tuesday had taken Nina with her to Arizona, where her mother lived in a cool, square cottage painted blue. Tuesday had even talked about moving there but had been concerned about the bugs in the house. She wanted to know which ones to fear, to learn about poisons and toxins and antidotes. She'd heard that scorpions climbed up walls and flung themselves into children's beds, that wasps caught in sheets on the laundry line and stung in the night. "I need to know what to be scared of," she'd told him on the phone. She'd used a playing card to knock a black widow into a Dixie cup. She'd freeze the bugs, then take them in a little tin that used to be a sewing kit to Poison Control, where she'd have them identified.

"I caught some fireflies for you tonight, but I guess I forgot them at the drive-in," Hud said. He thought of them dying, slowly losing their flicker in the olive jar. "Nina . . . we're out of gas, I guess. And I'm not real sure where we are. But see that dot of light over there?" He pointed to someplace far up the road. "I think we can walk over there, and maybe there'll be a phone."

Nina shrugged, and said nonchalantly, "Mom won't be mad. It could happen to anybody."

Hud took a flashlight from the glove compartment. Outside the car, he squatted so that Nina could crawl onto his back. She wrapped her legs around his waist, clasped her hands at his chest. With her warm breath on his neck, he thought he could walk for hours and hours. And he thought he might have to—the small dot of light was not growing. When Hud nearly tripped on some barbed wire at the edge of a cornfield, it was as if he could feel the danger in his ankles then, a tenseness, and he kept the beam of the flashlight low to the ground. After a while, Nina's grip loosened, and she was slipping, and he asked if she'd like him to carry her in his arms so she could sleep. He felt her nod her head against his.

In his arms, she was much heavier, and he tired quickly. He sat down to rest on the edge of a ditch. When he looked up for the light, it was gone; the family in the house had simply turned out their lights and gone to bed.

Let it happen, he thought. *Let's stay lost.* The summer sun could wear their skin away and bleach their bones. Experts would have to unlock their rib cages and untangle their skeletons. Then, in memory and punishment, the town could celebrate Halloween again, no matter what season of the year, dressing up in skull masks and glow-in-the-dark bone suits.

Nina scratched her ear in her sleep. As Hud ran his finger along her cheek, the bridge of her nose, her lips, he welcomed all the misery that would come in the morning for having kept her in his arms in the middle of nowhere. He felt brave only because Nina felt safe and protected enough to rest.

3.

▲▲▲▲▲▲▲▲▲▲▲▲

TUESDAY woke on the sofa,, blinking at the morning light, her shirtdress drenched in sweat. Scratching her head, which itched from the thick Aqua Net in her unraveling beehive, she stood and put her bare foot over the floor vent. She felt only a gust of tepid air. Twice in five days the air conditioner repairman had claimed to have fixed a Freon leak. She got a stomachache thinking of the expense of replacing the unit, and she began to list in her mind all the other fallibilities of her house. The unkempt branches of a tree would soon enough be scratching threateningly against the windows with any gust of winter wind. And the faulty wiring kept the house only halfway electrical.

This was something Tuesday did—she would stop a minute to concentrate on the most decrepit circumstances of her life. She'd close her eyes and immerse herself in the misery until she was druggy with unhappiness, until every obstacle seemed hazy with the impossibility of solution, and she'd drop, tired, into her sofa cushions. If it was just her, Tuesday wouldn't care about a house hot like an oven. If she was all alone, all she'd need was a tiny corner of a cold-water flat.

When she opened the window to glance outside at the air conditioner, she saw a girl's legs poking out from the thicket of mums planted alongside the house. Though the legs were long and thin, entirely un-Nina-like, Tuesday felt certain for a second that she'd just happened upon her daughter dead in the grass. Part of her had always been prepared for Nina to go suddenly and absolutely from her life. Some nights she'd be startled awake by the complete silence of the house, and she'd have to wake Nina with a soft shake and crawl into bed with her. Nina would stroke Tuesday's hair and whisper-sing a new song she'd memorized.

A butterfly landed on the leg blotchy with sunburn, and the girl, not dead after all, slapped at the startlingly sea-blue bug as if it was as useless as a mosquito. Tuesday stepped outside. "Millie," she said, seeing that the legs belonged to the girl who lived in the country but was always tumbling around town, the twelve-year-old with perpetually dirty knees who would sometimes sneak into the backyard to play with Nina and strip her Barbies naked. Millie wore a yellow tutu and ballerina slippers, and she lay next to candy spilled from a plastic, pumpkin-shaped bucket.

"Did you take Nina's candy?" Tuesday said. She noticed Nina's open window and recognized the bucket and its contents from when Tuesday took her trick-or-treating around the block before the costume party. Millie sat up then, her eyes heavy-lidded, her head bobbing on her neck. She seemed startled out of some stupor, looking all caught-in-the-act.

"Nina's not in her room," Millie said. Her skin was the white-blue of skim milk, her breath smelling slightly of chemicals. "This was on her bed." She handed Tuesday a crumpled piece of paper, then stood, her tutu droopy, and stumbled away, nearly tripping over the loose laces of her slippers.

Before Tuesday even read the note, she knew it was from Hud, recognized the skinny, spiky letters of his serial-killer scrawl. Tuesday rushed to the open window, anxious to touch Nina, to feel Nina's back minutely rise and fall with her slow breath as she slept so late. She reached into the window and, pushing at the empty puff of the goose-down duvet on the bed, she realized how easily any passing stranger could grab Nina by the hair and whisk her away with nothing much more than a flick of the wrist.

Deep in her heart, she knew Hud would never vanish with their daughter, though he wouldn't be throwing away much of a life, as she saw it. All he loved about the town was the flea market on the courthouse lawn on Saturdays. Trashy teen-aged girls gathered in the grass at the steps of the bandstand where he sat to play his guitar and sing the songs he'd originally written for Tuesday. Tuesday sometimes worked a face-painting table at the flea market, painting unicorns and daisies on the cheeks of the children, and these girls, their dirty hair stinking with smoke, would walk up in their ratty tube tops and request that Tuesday paint little hearts and daggers, or their boyfriends' names in gothic letters, on their chests and skinny upper arms. They'd sit giggling as Tuesday worked her brush begrudgingly across their baby-pink skin, the girls tipsy off whatever soft booze—the melon liqueur or wine cooler—they drank from a lunch-box thermos, using a Twizzler for a straw.

When I get Nina back, Tuesday thought, picking up a Tootsie Pop from the ground, unwrapping it, and tapping it against her teeth, *I'll let her have the run of the place.* She would let Nina drink Pepsi for breakfast, let her sleep naked in the sandbox. "Why would I go anywhere with you?" Nina would tell Hud as she painted her toenails any color, even a garish hooker-red.

I hate him, she thought. Walking quickly toward the town square, where the flea market would already be under way, she ducked the toilet paper hanging from some of the trees and twisting in the hot breeze like streamers. Even when she loved Hud madly, she would fantasize about his death. Maybe not fantasize, but she would imagine what it would be like. *He put her through a lot,* people would say, marveling at her stoicism, *but she was so devoted.* They'd all call her the Young Widow Smith and would feel a thump of sympathy when they'd catch sight of her in the months after, wearing sunglasses in the winter and polyester scarves over her hair, resembling Barbara Stanwyck on her way to an illicit encounter.

As Tuesday approached the courthouse lawn, chewing on the hard candy of the Tootsie pop, she saw that Hud's small but regular audience had already gathered at the bandstand steps. One of the girls wore curlers and distractedly pulled at a piece of frayed thread at the edge of the American flag draped across a rail of the gazebo. "Where is he?" Tuesday asked, and the girl shrugged. This was the one who loved Hud the most—Tuesday had watched her once. She had rested her head on another girl's shoulder as she listened to Hud sing. Later, she had come to Tuesday's table and asked her to paint on her throat as many words as she could fit from the lyric, "I taste the tart wild plum on your lips," which Tuesday knew from a song Hud had written about a summer afternoon they'd spent at a lake years before, back when they were a couple of love-struck babies.

"When he sings," the girl had said as Tuesday painted, the stretched skin of her neck twitching as she spoke, causing the blue letters to smear, "his voice is so strong, I can feel it shiver my chest." But that wasn't enough for the girl. Tuesday could tell she was thinking deep by the way her tongue clicked a little, her whistle wet with more to say. "It's so strong in my chest, he can change the beat in my heart, make it beat to the beat of the song." *Ridiculous,* Tuesday thought. Hud's singing voice was weak and full of cracks. It would break at a song's most emotional moment, obscuring key words, sometimes obliterating all meaning.

"Have you seen Hud? Or Nina?" Tuesday asked Ozzie Yates, who sold peaches from the back of the pickup he backed up to the edge of the lawn. Tuesday and Ozzie were old friends, and Tuesday's son, Gatling, had loved Ozzie's daughter, Charlotte.

"No," Ozzie said, winking, "I've not seen Hud. And I'm damn near close to tears about it." Ozzie and Hud shared a notorious animosity for each other, a friendly hatred that bordered on the sexy. Ozzie, in his dirty, loose-fit Levis and Western shirt all unsnapped down the front of his hairy chest, had been the one she had imagined being alone with when she was still lying next to Hud every night, scheming ways to ruin everything.

Ozzie took a pale yellow, nearly white peach from a basket and held it to Tuesday's cheek, touching the gentle fuzz to her skin. "How much for it?" she said. She took the fruit, running her thumb across its light bruises and its few patches of orange freckles.

"It's on the house," he said, and Tuesday smiled and walked away. Ozzie depressed her terribly sometimes, even when they just stood there negotiating the price of peaches. He'd once had a pretty wife who died of a swift illness, leaving him to raise Charlotte alone. Though Ozzie was not at all judgmental, she sensed something pleading in his wet eyes, like he wanted to scold her for so blindly letting her family fall apart.

Tuesday walked on down the rows of tables of castoff notions and novelties, still asking about Hud and Nina. She stopped at Lily Rollow's table and dipped her fingers into the teacups full of jewelry. Lily and her sister ran an antique shop in the country; the sister, Mabel, gave better bargains. Lily was cranky—she was pregnant and freshly divorced and only twenty years old. She sat in a fragile-looking lawn chair with a broken weave, a handheld battery-operated fan blowing her bangs up. "Who are you supposed to be?" Lily asked.

Tuesday touched at her hair, remembering she was still in last night's costume. "Catherine Deneuve in *Mississippi Mermaid*," she said.

"You're so funny," Lily said with a chuckle.

People often said that to Tuesday. But Tuesday didn't think of herself as funny at all, hadn't told so much as a tired joke in years. "Yeah," she told Lily. "I'm a regular Henny Youngman."

If anything, she was completely unfunny. She used to be funny, but she hadn't liked it. A woman wants to be thought mysterious and tragic. *I cry my eyes out most nights,* she wanted to object. *I listen to Roberta Flack and get sauced on hard cider and conk out, useless, around midnight.*

"It's adjustable," Lily pointed out as Tuesday watched the glass of a mood ring on her pinky cloud over from a peacock-feather blue. "Fifty cents."

Tuesday wanted to buy the ring for Nina, but she only had a quarter in the pocket of her dress. As she dug for more change, her fingers ran across a few hexagonal happy pills the Widow Bosanko had pressed into the palm of her hand the other afternoon during Nina's birthday party. She'd been carrying them around ever since. While a group of neighborhood brats had batted at a Raggedy Ann piñata, Hud had sauntered in holding a beer bottle at his side, with a girl's rabbit-fur coat he'd ordered from a catalog. Nina had worn the coat outside all day, stumbling, nearly fainting from the heat, her fair hair dark with sweat. "Mother's little helper," the Widow had whispered, administering the pills to Tuesday in a handshake, the wooden cherries of her bracelet rattling.

Tuesday wanted to swallow the pills now, but she remembered how a psychiatrist had put Gatling on prescriptions once, mood drugs that made him dopey and sluggish and trembled his hands. But for a while it had been a relief having Gatling so docile and curled up on her sofa watching afternoon reruns of *The Rockford Files* and *McMillan and Wife*.

Lily accepted the quarter as payment for the ring, and Tuesday walked on to Hud's building. The buzzer, she knew, didn't buzz, so she picked up some crumbled pieces of brick on the sidewalk and tossed them up to tap against the upstairs windows. *Where is my family?* she thought, noticing her reflection in the window of the defunct shoe repair shop. She pulled the one remaining false eyelash from her lid, then ran her long press-on nails through her hair, combing out her beehive. *When you're all alone in the world, you only have yourself to worry about,* she thought. *But when you have people, their tragedies are your tragedies. Your potential for misery is doubled, tripled, quadrupled.*

Then she looked past her reflection to the shoes that remained on a shelf. The shop owners had just up and closed one day, after committing their thirty-year-old autistic son to an institution. They retired to Oregon, leaving behind some repaired shoes still uncollected, others still unrepaired. Tuesday saw one of her own strappy sandals that she'd forgotten she owned. The thin black ankle strap that had broken loose was now perfectly reattached, and the shoe sat waiting to step off into an elegant evening, high-heeled and pristine, its toe scuffs polished away. It wasn't the type of shoe she'd wear, so she hadn't even missed it, didn't even know where its match was. She'd bought the shoes a few years before, when she and Hud were trying to save their marriage. Every other weekend or so, they would dress up and drive to the casinos across the river from Omaha. While Hud played blackjack after dinner with loosened necktie, Tuesday, in her black cocktail dress, would sit alone at a table in the lounge sipping chocolate martinis and listening to a woman who impersonated Barbara Streisand, Tina Turner, and Karen Carpenter. Those evenings, Tuesday thought, weren't as bad as they sounded. They were nice, actually.

Tuesday rubbed at the glass of her mood ring as she headed back home, hoping to work its mud-colored froth into a shade of pink. As she turned the corner onto her street, she slowed her steps, giving Hud a better chance to sneak Nina back into her bed. Ghosts knotted together from pillow cases hung from porch eaves. A scarecrow, its stuffing beaten out of it, lay in a heap in the middle of the street.

In her driveway now were her father's Caddy and her sister's VW bug. When she saw Mrs. Katt, the neighbor, walk up to the porch, she began to panic. Mrs. Katt would show up at any moment of despair with a can of Folgers, and she'd scrub your kitchen while you convalesced with your family in another room. You'd sit in your pajamas, you'd play rummy, waiting for some news or some fever to break, and become somewhat eased by the heavy scent of cinnamon as Mrs. Katt heated an offering in the stove. Tuesday had a cupboard full of Mrs. Katt's plates and tureens she needed to return, all with the woman's name on a piece of masking tape on the bottom.

Tuesday quit worrying when she heard the loud discord of the out-of-tune piano as somebody tumbled their fingers across the keys. Hud was the only one who ever played the piano, which had been shoved onto the screened-in back porch, and she began to hear his voice rising above the whir of the broken air conditioner. She didn't want to be, but she was glad to hear him singing in her house. She thought of one beautiful song Hud had played for her on the piano on a wet October night. As the rain *tip-tipped* against the screens, she rocked a sleeping Nina in the old chair they'd had since their first apartment. The joints of the rocking chair squeaked and quivered, and Hud sang softly a song he made up on the spot, about what it felt like to dream at night about a girl like Tuesday.

Pressing her forehead against the screen of the porch door, Tuesday watched Hud entertain her father and the Widow and her older sister, Rose, named for the shock of her father's red hair she'd been born with, and Mrs. Katt. They all stood or sat sipping coffee from Tuesday's best cups, swaying to Hud's song, which seemed to be about a brokenhearted father putting his children to bed. Rose and Red sat in the nearly wrecked wicker chairs, small plates of Mrs. Katt's crumb cake balanced on their knees. Everyone's eyes were on Nina, who did an interpretive dance in the middle of the small room, just behind the piano bench. Nina linked her fingers above her head, closed her eyes, and turned on the ball of one foot in an approximation of a pirouette. She then quickly and awkwardly moved into a jazz singer's slo-mo hip shimmy and snaked her arms around in front of herself. Nina's dancing was silly and pretty all at once, and Tuesday closed her eyes, mesmerized by her daughter.

Then Nina screamed, startled out of her hypnotic dance by the sight of Tuesday's dark shadow at the screen. Nina stood there, both hands tight at her mouth. Hud stopped playing, and everyone looked, alarmed, toward the door.

"Mommy!" Nina said when she realized it was only Tuesday. She ran to the screen and opened it, then hugged Tuesday's legs. "Oh, you won't believe what happened," Nina said, speaking in a rush. "It's not Daddy's fault, really it's not," she said. "Really it's not. The car. It's the car's fault. The car just up and took a shit on him."

Tuesday finger-thumped the top of Nina's head. "You know I don't want you talking like that," she said. She looked around the room as everyone avoided her eyes. They looked into their coffee cups, or out the windows of the porch, suddenly embarrassed for having enjoyed Hud's company. Hud just sat hunched at the piano, pushing down slowly on this key, then that, making no music. Rose pinched at a run in the ankle of her stocking. *Stockings,* thought Tuesday. *Now, how about that. Practically crack-of-dawn Saturday morning and there she sits in pricey shoes and her best light-yellow summer dress.* Rose always did have a thing for Hud. Tuesday could smell the stench of Rose's perfume, some designer knockoff she ordered by the vat on the Internet.

"Honeycomb," Tuesday said to Nina, bending over to kiss the top of her head, "would you go to your room and wait for Mommy? I'll be in in a minute to tell you how much you worried me."

"OK," Nina said, walking away with her head lowered.

"So how'd everyone hear about Hud's little party this morning?" Tuesday said. "His little party here in my house?"

"We were up at the flea market," the Widow said. "People said your hair was a mess and you were looking for Nina."

"Don't make a federal case, Day," Rose said, sharing a smirk with Hud and crossing her legs. "Everything's fine."

"You stink," Tuesday said, feeling mean toward everyone there. "Where the hell did you get that cologne? Truck stop?"

"Oh, girls," Red said. "Let's be sweet."

Rose laughed through her nose, rolled her eyes. "Shows you how much you know," she said. "It's Shoot the Moon you're smelling."

"Oh, is that what that is?" the Widow said, clearly impressed. "I thought maybe that's what."

"Got it at Marshall Field's that last time in Chicago," Rose told the Widow, uncrossing her legs, then recrossing them. "I'll get you some the next time I go back."

"Oh, honey, I'd kiss you all over," the Widow said.

Rose would never have paid the $100 a bottle for Shoot the Moon, Tuesday knew. She probably just tore an ad from a fashion magazine and rubbed the scented page against her throat in the car on the way over.

When Hud began tapping out "Chopsticks" on the piano, Tuesday reached over to slam down the lid over the keys. Hud snapped his hands back just in time and jumped at the loud noise of the fallen lid. "Damn, Day," he said, looking up at her with that baffled, what-the-hell-did-I-ever-do-to-you? look he'd mastered years before. With that look, so carefully maneuvered he must have practiced in a mirror, he always effectively made Tuesday feel like the biggest bitch that'd ever walked upright. In his lovely blue eyes, with that look, were kindness and a boy's gentle confusion. Gatling had inherited Hud's counterfeit innocence, had started working that same look way too young.

"One of these days I'll run away with her myself," Tuesday said, remembering the peach in her pocket. She pulled it out and pressed at a soft part of the fruit, trying to keep from crying again. "I'll drop a match on this whole house of sticks as I leave. You'll lose everything. The piano, your songbooks, all the crap you left behind. And we'll be nowhere to be found."

"You were just inches from setting the place on fire last night," Hud said, whispering just loudly enough for everyone in the room to hear. "You had fallen asleep with a cigarette still smoking, burning a hole in the sofa. Who knows how big a fire you would've made if I hadn't shown up? I, for one, don't particularly want a little burn victim for a little girl."

"Cigarettes," the Widow Bosanko said, sighing, shaking her head. Mr. Bosanko had died of lung cancer.

Tuesday put the peach back in her pocket and left the room. She didn't feel on the verge of tears anymore. Hud always took an argument just one step too far. He could so easily have her in the palm of his hand, right there along with Rose and the Widow, but then he'd say something too godawful. If he'd just left it at "Who knows how big a fire . . ." But then he had to turn Nina into a burn victim, erasing away all her darling features, her tiny, perfect nose and soft lashes and those lips of pale, pale pink.

In the bathroom she took off her dress and leaned her head over the side of the tub to rinse out her stiff hair. When she turned the water off, she heard that Hud had gone back to performing the rest of his song. Tuesday wrapped her wet head in a towel, stepping into the hallway wearing only the matching silk bra and underwear patterned with blue bunnies that Rose had given her last Christmas.

After pulling on a short tartan skirt and a t-shirt and grabbing her face-painting kit, Tuesday went to Nina's room. Nina sat on the bed dressing her paper doll in a paper ball gown, and Tuesday sat beside her. She touched the fringe of Nina's faux-leather vest. "You can wear this today too if you want," Tuesday said.

"Good," Nina said.

"Don't ever leave me in the middle of the night, please," Tuesday said. "Not even with your father. He's full of evil schemes. I hate him."

"No, you don't," Nina said, taking the tiny comb from her plastic purse, then running it through Tuesday's hair.

"Yes, I do. Ouch. My hair's all snaggy." She took the comb from Nina and did it herself. "I hate him, and so will you someday. And you'll hate me too, someday, I suppose."

"No, I won't," Nina whined, scrunching up her nose and chin with offense. "You don't know."

Tuesday lifted the torn screen of the window. "Let's go," she whispered, and together they crept out onto the lawn as Hud got to an emotional part of the song that involved a kind of pained bellowing. Tuesday lifted Nina into the handlebar basket of her bicycle, hooked the face-painting kit to the back, and rode away, the bike shaky on its wheels. Nina sat high in the basket in her cowgirl suit, the fresh peach cradled in the cup of her two hands.

4 .

︴︴︴︴︴

H I S thumb in a thimble, Ozzie sat on the open tailgate of his pickup. He sewed to distract himself these days, repairing years of tears in old trousers and shirts and moth-eaten sweaters. He had taught himself embroidery from a book, and he stitched a rose into the point of a collar of one of Charlotte's childhood blouses.

When he had left his house that morning with his few baskets of peaches collected from the tiny orchard in his backyard, Charlotte had yet to come home from the drive-in. Her staying out all night wasn't all that unusual anymore, but she claimed complete innocence, spoke of all-night prayer meetings and spiritual sweats at midnight and meditation in country ditches. "Junior's a good boy," she told him, "not like Gatling." Charlotte spent most of her late afternoons lying sullen and lanky on the living room sofa, letting Junior kneel beside her and talk in her ear. In a hard whisper, the boy seduced her easily with preaching of biblical catastrophe and plague. She was at an age to be prone to any sort of depravity, Ozzie's neighbors said. A girl Charlotte's age, they said from their front porches and window perches, a girl so long without a mother, looks for divine undoing, for the kind of violent, snaky salvation a boy like Junior promises.

Ozzie's fingers were a bit too big for the delicate embroidery, and he stopped a moment and rested his hands in his lap. Ozzie worked with stained glass, repairing church windows from county to county. His burned and scarred hands, with the grooves in the skin, were lately beginning to resemble his windows of glass shards. He used to be much more careful handling the melted lead for the soldering.

Though the death of Jenny, Charlotte's mother, three years before, was certainly one of the reasons for Charlotte's newfound religion and her skanky, psalm-reciting boyfriend, Ozzie recognized his own blame. For years he'd brought Charlotte along to the churches old and new, country and city, to remove the damaged stained-glass windows. As she waited, she stood at the pulpits and pounded her fists, faking blustery sermons, or baptized her rag dolls, dipping their yarn hair into the fonts. Then the windows, for weeks, sat in his studio as he intricately pieced back together a broken glass Jesus or nameless saint. When the sun was at the back windows, the powdery colors filled the room, touching Charlotte's cheeks and hands as she played on the floor with the cat.

"Charlotte's on the other side of the square," said a neighbor as she purchased a sackful of peaches. The neighbor had teenagers of her own and spoke with a conspiratorial hush.

Ozzie poked his needle into the cuff of his shirt and walked through the flea market, scanning the crowd. He found Charlotte, still in her geisha-girl costume and wearing what looked to be pink fangs in her open mouth, lying in the grass and sleeping with her head on Junior's chest. Junior slept as well, his hand in Charlotte's hair. Junior was certainly not unlikable. He was as handsome as a drowned-rat kind of a boy could be, with thick black hair greased back. He carried a clarinet around with him, saying that he was teaching himself complicated jazz tunes like "So What" and "Undecided." Charlotte met him when he worked as an apprentice at an ironworks. Above the garage door of the building was a plaster statue of Christ in an iron cage wrought with curlicues and spikes. Ozzie could just see Charlotte penitent in the doorway watching the boy stand among sparks and blue flame.

Charlotte and Junior slept next to a quilt—for the previous few flea markets, Charlotte had been selling off the stuff of her childhood. All the long-abandoned dolls and books of fairy tales and framed photos of childhood friends had been spread out across the quilt and marked with bottom-barrel prices, and Ozzie had been her best customer—last week he'd bought a tin bird he'd bought for her years before, and some faded candy necklaces. Now, next to the few things she had yet to sell, was a sign that said, "Take whatever you want. It's all FREE."

Ozzie recalled the words of Charlotte's high school guidance counselor, who he had visited one recent afternoon: *Don't worry much*, the woman had said, *until she starts to give her things away.* A sign of suicidal tendencies, it seemed.

Ozzie kicked gently at Charlotte's side—he could almost imagine his daughter and Junior sleepy from poison-spiked Kool-Aid.

"Daddy," Charlotte said, unalarmed, sitting up to stretch.

Ozzie grabbed the box next to the quilt and collected the few things that remained. "Pickup's parked over there," Ozzie said. "We're going home."

"I'm glad you're here, Mr. Yates," Junior said, standing and brushing the dried grass off his jeans. Ozzie saw Junior give Charlotte a wink and a nod, granting her permission to obey her father. The gesture turned Ozzie's stomach. "I'd like to discuss something with you," Junior said, his eyes on Charlotte as she walked away.

Though Junior was soft-spoken, Ozzie knew there was no refusing him. Junior had no knives, no gun, and was too slight in build to pose any physical threat. His command of the family was simply the result of Charlotte's devotion. Charlotte's fast love for him had turned her feral and easily spooked, and Ozzie was afraid if he made one wrong move, she'd dart.

"Actually, I want to talk to you too," Ozzie said before Junior spoke again. Ozzie picked up a Slinky from the box and let it coil and uncoil in his hand. "I don't want you to see my daughter so much anymore." He looked deeper into the box, his weak demand dropping off. A spark of sunlight glinted off the tip of the boy's cowboy boot.

"Oh, Mr. Yates," Junior said, smiling, shrugging. "'The glory of young men is their strength, and the honor of old men is their gray hair.'"

"I'll call the authorities," Ozzie said. He pushed back the bangs of his hair, none of it gray that he had ever noticed. "There's a thing called statutory rape, and it's very illegal."

"I don't think you will, Mr. Yates." Junior stepped in and put his hand to the back of Ozzie's head. He leaned over, whispering, " 'For you bear with anyone if he enslaves you, if he devours you, if he takes advantage of you, if he exalts himself, if he hits you in the face.' " Just the sound of Junior's voice brought to Ozzie's mind scratchy black woodcut images of hordes of children, their eyes lidded with pestilence, of screaming angels with burnt wings, of buzzards and dead lions, all of which the boy had described to Charlotte as his picture of the end of the world.

Ozzie looked up again, his eyes only inches from the boy's. "Don't you have any words of your own?" he said. But he understood something about Junior. Ozzie had had his own brief bout with religion in the months after Jenny's death—he'd wanted to sink into the open arms of the church and become disoriented by the archaic recitations of proverbs and creeds. The congregation, their Bibles and hymnals held to their faces, spoke a dark language of rapture and damnation. Ozzie had wanted no ease with the world, or easeful words to speak with. He'd wanted to be ruined for life.

Junior smiled with only half his mouth, a wicked smile, you'd call it, and he snapped a flame from his open Zippo. He lit a hand-rolled cigarette and said, "We're getting married, Mr. Yates. That's what I wanted to tell you. And don't go thinking that she's too young, because she's not." He leaned in again, and Ozzie felt his hot breath on his cheek. " 'Her lips drip honey,'" he said. "'Honey and milk are under her tongue.'" As he slipped a card into the chest pocket of Ozzie's shirt, Ozzie shoved Junior's shoulders. Junior stumbled backward, his arms flailing for balance, until he fell into the tall base of a memorial statue that the Chamber of Commerce had installed on the courthouse lawn in honor of soldiers who'd fought in Vietnam.

"Mr. Yates," Junior said, getting back up, a spot of blood blooming just beneath his eye from the scratch of the tip of an angel's stone wing, "we're told, 'A tranquil heart is life to the body, but passion is rottenness to the bones.'"

"Rotten bones," Ozzie mumbled. He turned and walked away with the cardboard box of Charlotte's things.

Ozzie took from his pocket what Junior had put in: a picture of Christ, a very contemporary representation of him as pretty as a blue-eyed young girl with his long hair partly braided. He was entirely nude and nailed to the cross, blood flowing along the sinewy muscle of his arms, his godly schlong mostly hidden by shadow. *His Pain, Your Gain* was written at the bottom of the card. Ozzie wondered where the boy had even come across such a picture; perhaps priests handed them out in the street to seduce young people into church.

Charlotte sat in the truck, waiting, reading a tiny green Gideon's Bible with a magnifying glass. Ozzie got in with the box, then drove away without closing the tailgate. He ignored the light thumping of the peaches as they spilled and rolled across the truck bed.

At a stop sign, he leaned toward Charlotte and smelled something sugary on her breath. Didn't they used to say that if a baby's breath smelled sweet, it portended a terrible sickness? As new parents, Ozzie and Jenny had been forewarned of all sorts of infanticides. When Charlotte was first born, Jenny banished Simp, the old tom, to the studio out back. Ozzie had never heard of a cat's attraction to a sleeping child's breath, but Jenny had been warned by all the old ladies up and down the street of the danger of such suffocation.

"Did you know," Charlotte said, barely looking up from her little green book, "that you can break a snake's back if you don't handle it correctly? And there are whole churches of people who mix themselves strychnine drinks because the Bible says, 'Drink poison and ye shall live.' They call it a salvation cocktail." Lightly, she delivered this information, this hint at how deeply a religious fervor had infected her.

"On my way back to the truck just now," Ozzie said, "I remembered that afternoon we found that bat in the house. The one we had in the attic. Remember that? Your mom made me catch it in a coffee can so we could let it out in the country. So the three of us drove a few miles down a road . . . the bat crying all the way."

Charlotte, clearly bored by the fact that he didn't make more of her mention of snake handling and poison drinking, rolled her eyes and returned to the New Testament.

Ozzie saw that Charlotte's lips and fingertips were berry-stained, skeletons of dry leaves caught in her hair. Her scent of sweetness had dissolved into the smell of smoke, but not cigarette smoke, smoke like from twigs and bark. She seemed weakened by her thinking about the night. *Keep a tranquil heart,* he wanted to warn her. *Passion is rottenness to the bones.*

On the corner of Elm and Oak sat one of the older churches in town, a squat, homely thing of gray stone, but with a few majestic windows depicting intricate biblical scenes. Ozzie had long wanted to get his hands on the glass of Grace Lutheran—the windows looked to have been shoddily repaired in the past, and poorly maintained, with some of the lighter-colored pieces—like the opalescent skirts of an angel—having grown dim with years of dust. And if he wasn't mistaken, the belly of the whale was made of what looked to be rotten ruby—a rare antique red.

Ozzie pulled around the corner and stopped the truck a fair distance from the church. He opened the truck door, then picked up a library copy of *Franny and Zooey* from the box. He dropped the book into Charlotte's lap.

"I've read this," she said, pushing the book aside.

"And you love it," he shouted, seethed, really. "Read it again." He then took from the box the paper-thin plastic Halloween mask Charlotte had worn three years before, when she'd trick-or-treated as Spider-Man. That fall, the first after Jenny's death, he'd put together an elaborate Rapunzel costume for her for a junior high party—gold and silver thread stitched into a blue velvet cloak, a blond wig with a thick braid that wrapped around her waist and fell to her feet. But at the last minute Charlotte refused the Rapunzel costume, and Ozzie took her to the grocery store, where she bought the Spider-Man mask with matching plastic smock, the only costume left on the shelf, and went off to the party looking like some hopeless urchin.

Walking back to the church, keeping close to the row of trees that lined the street, Ozzie put the mask over his face, pulling the little string of elastic over his head. With his other hand, he picked up a pumpkin from the edge of someone's yard and carried it by its stem. His heavy breaths were noisy against the flimsy mask. He squinted to see through the slim eyeholes.

The damage he intended to do wouldn't be serious, he told himself. And it would cost the church nothing—Ozzie had every intention of volunteering his services for the repairs, and footing the bill for any replacement glass. The church would chalk it all up to vandals, and Ozzie could finally drive by the old place with a sense of peace. He'd no longer have to see all that sunlight muddied by dirt trapped in the glass, or see how the window sagged and chipped from its own weight.

Crouching in a deep shadow, Ozzie lifted the pumpkin above his head and aimed for a warped sash in order to do minimal harm. The pumpkin crashed against the window, shattering just enough of the glass to require careful repair, and Ozzie bolted from the site before the broken rind and guts of the pumpkin even hit the ground.

Once back inside the truck, he pushed the mask up off his face to rest atop his head. As he drove off, Charlotte, who had seen none of her father's destruction, reached into the box and picked up some x-ray specs. "You know Mrs. diFanta from down the street?" she said, putting on the glasses. "She witnessed a sun miracle. That's when you look in the sky and see the sun dancing. That's how she went blind." She wiggled her hands in front of her face, as if she could see through her skin.

Ozzie looked straight ahead but watched his daughter in the rearview mirror. For years Ozzie had been looking at Charlotte, studying her, certain there'd come a time when he'd never see her again. Her absence from his life had always seemed just seconds away. And now it was as if he couldn't see her at all, not even when looking right at her. Instead, he saw her clearly, so clearly, at thirteen years old, in the moments just before he told her that her mother had died. He had waited for her in front of the house and, with both dread and relief, watched her approach. It had begun to rain, and Charlotte struggled and rushed down the street on her roller skates, her open umbrella flailing about as she tried to keep her balance.

ⵝⵝ
I N all the years Tuesday had been smitten with Ozzie Yates, she'd only ever kissed him on the stage of the community theater. She'd played Frankie to his Johnny in *Frankie and Johnny in the Clair de Lune* a few summers before Jenny took sick. Tuesday particularly remembered one evening's late rehearsal when they'd waited out a hailstorm, backstage, sipping too-strong coffee, sitting on the lumpy poppy-print sofa that had been used in the theater's every living room stage set of the last twenty years. Tuesday and Ozzie had known each other since high school, but that night was the first he'd heard that her father had named her after Tuesday Weld. "Ah, the Marlon Brando of women," Ozzie had said. He had to tell her he was quoting from *The Motel Chronicles* by Sam Shepard, and after the first show, Ozzie gave her a copy of the Shepard book as a gift, wrapped in the colorful print of the previous Sunday's funnies. Hud hadn't even given her a single rose on opening night.

So she knew Ozzie, despite his Spider-Man mask, by his long legs and the dark curls that just touched the top of his collar, by the way he kept the cuffs of his shirt sleeves unsnapped. She had been on her way back to the flea market, with Nina in the basket of her bicycle, but stopped the bike at the curb by the church when she saw the pumpkin flung. She didn't even realize she was giggling until Nina looked back, her eyes wide with shock, after Ozzie dashed away. "What's funny?" Nina scolded.

"Nothing," Tuesday said.

"Then why are you laughing?" Nina said.

"Sometimes I laugh at things that aren't funny," she said. What explanation was there? She had caught sight of an old friend so down for so long with heartache and grief, doing something sudden and dumb. It was hilarious. *You should be laughing your head off,* she wanted to tell Nina.

"He broke the angel with blue feathers," Nina said, her voice hushed with reverence. A few years before, on the courthouse lawn, Nina had tensed at the sight of the sculpture of a stone angel on a podium kneeling in remorse, its enormous gray wingspan casting a long, thin, late-afternoon shadow across the grass. Nina had shrieked, as if the angel were poised to swoop down and scoop her up. In the days that followed, Tuesday took her out to seek angels—they spotted one painted on the side of a barn, another carved into a tombstone turning to dust in an abandoned cemetery, a glass one with a gold trumpet in Rose's china cabinet. Nina's fears abated, she and Tuesday picnicked beneath the stained-glass angel with blue-tinted wings in the church window, stuffing themselves with fried chicken legs and macaroni.

They rode directly to Ozzie's house, and Charlotte answered the door, pushing back her cuticles with an orange stick. She wore a t-shirt and pajama bottoms, her face scrubbed clean, leaving her looking pudgy-cheeked and babyish. It was funny for Tuesday to think of all the damage this raggedy thing did to her home only months before, when her son used to date her. Tuesday missed seeing Ozzie regularly, when he'd come to the house distraught over Charlotte kept out too late. Tuesday had secretly loved his midnight arguments with Hud, when he'd threaten to have Gatling arrested if his motherless little girl wasn't soon returned to the safety of her pink canopy bed. Once Ozzie had even bloodied Hud's nose, and as Hud, too drunk to stand that night, tried to pick himself up from the porch floor, Ozzie whispered to Tuesday, "I'm not mad at *you.*" She blushed at the satisfying absolution, feeling as if she somehow conspired against the errant men of her home.

"Nin, darling," Charlotte said, faux demure, bending at the waist, pinky lifted, to kiss Nina on the cheek.

"Lot," Nina said, kissing back. She mimicked Charlotte's tea-party snootiness, but Tuesday could tell Nina wanted to leap like a wild child into Charlotte's arms. When she dated Gatling, Charlotte took Nina out for sisterly afternoons shopping thrift stores in Grand Island, and Nina would come home looking a fright in a faded, powder-blue Hello Kitty baby tee, her little-girl paunch peeking out the bottom of it, or shaky-legged on a pair of platform clogs three sizes too big.

"I've missed you," Charlotte told Nina, and she reached into a cardboard box on the floor next to the door. She took from it a barrette with a cloth daisy and clipped it into Nina's hair. "I want you to have that."

"Tell her thank you," Tuesday said.

"I love it," Nina said, trying to see it through the tops of her eyes, reaching up to touch the daisy's frayed petals.

"Dad's upstairs," Charlotte told Tuesday. "Go on up. He just got in the tub, and he'll be in it for hours. He just sits there crying, drinking pink Andre, and turning pruney." She tapped her orange stick on the top of Nina's head. "You and me are going to go wash that dirty, dirty hair of yours. I have a recipe for some shampoo that I clipped from an old *Cosmo* I found at the Salvation Army. It calls for beer and egg."

"Ick," Nina said happily.

Her hair was dirty, it was true; Tuesday hadn't washed it for her in days. Nina normally hated to have her head touched, so she went through life with rats and tangles and natural curls that sagged like she was some gutter-drunk Shirley Temple. *I should be turned in to Social Services,* Tuesday thought, plucking a nettle from Nina's hair, charmed by Nina's messiness. *I should be denied all motherly privileges.*

Nina handed Tuesday the peach, its skin damp and warm from Nina's palms, then followed Charlotte into the kitchen. Upstairs, Tuesday stopped to listen at the bathroom door. She knocked gently. "I saw what you did," she said.

"Come on in," Ozzie said. "Most of myself is behind the shower curtain."

Ozzie soaked in the soapy water, the Spider-Man mask pushed up to the top of his head, his body halfway concealed by the once-clear shower curtain now opaque from mildew and water stain. Tuesday had seen Ozzie naked once, when he was eighteen and she was sixteen. They had all gone skinny-dipping at the river. Tuesday and her sister, Rose, nude, sunned themselves self-consciously on an inflatable raft, their arms carefully placed, legs carefully crossed, positioning themselves to cast modest shadows. They pretended not to stare at Ozzie and the way his muscles moved, the way drops caught and glistened in the hair of his body. He stood waist-high in the river, trying to lift his laughing Jenny in his arms to dunk her, headfirst, into the drink.

"You didn't see what you think you saw," Ozzie said, writing Tuesday's name in the steam on the shower curtain.

Tuesday had a seat on the closed toilet lid and took a swig from Ozzie's bottle of pink champagne gone flat, then another swig. "What do I think I saw?"

"Wipe the steam from the TV screen, would you, doll face?" Ozzie asked, handing her a dry washcloth. A tiny portable black-and-white with tinfoil on its antenna sat in the sink. "That cougar's about to rip the big wings off that ugly bird."

Tuesday offered him the peach, and Ozzie took his straight razor from the edge of the tub and sliced at the fruit. He held the razor and a piece of peach up to Tuesday's lips, and she ate the fruit off the blade. She felt a little dizzy, and her eyes watered, just from her few sips of Andre, the steaminess of the room, and the heavy scent of Ozzie's soap. And from the lush of the peach, she guessed. The soap had a wet-wood smell that made her nostalgic and that she could taste on her tongue, reminding her of her grade school band practice and the reeds of her alto sax.

"You think you saw me ruining something, but, see, I was actually saving that window," he said. "They've just been letting it crack and warp. I've offered several times to work on it, but they don't care enough."

"Hud took Nina in the middle of the night," Tuesday said, anxious to cast aspersions on her ex. Ozzie had always been willing to hear the worst about Hud, even back when everybody was everybody's friend. "While I slept. Didn't bring her back until after daylight."

Ozzie rolled his eyes and muttered. "But I wasn't all that worried," she said, suddenly feeling guilty. Steam hot on her cheek, Tuesday remembered a Christmas morning of a few years before, Gatling and Nina off in Phoenix with their grandmother, as Hud and Tuesday worked at their marriage. They'd had a moody bath together, Tuesday lying back against Hud's chest, drinking a beer at 10 A.M. They listened to a scratchy bootleg of Lucinda Williams singing a Hank Williams song. "It wasn't like he didn't leave a note. I knew he'd bring her back. It was just kind of unnerving. The poor guy's still in love with me after all, I think."

"Love," Ozzie said. "That's all the motivation a guy needs to wreck everything." He rubbed his bar of soap against the stubble of his chin, working up a lather, then picked up a shard of broken mirror from a tray of aftershaves and hair tonics at the side of the tub. In the little bit of mirror, Tuesday could see Ozzie's eye and his long black lashes. She loved the sound of the scratch of the blade against his chin, and, for a minute, she missed having men in her house.

Tuesday licked at sweat that dripped down her cheek to her lip and watched the wildlife show on the TV—two cheetah kittens wrestled and hissed. "Everybody's air conditioner is breaking down," she said. "I saw two repair trucks just on the short ride over here."

"The kids are huffing," Ozzie said. "They like to unscrew the valve with the Freon to get a whiff of it. Sometimes they pass out from it. But what the hell else do the little addicts have to do around here?"

Poor Millie, Tuesday thought, thinking of what a fright that girl would grow up to be. But she was actually relieved that there might not be anything seriously wrong with her air conditioner. She considered what she would buy with the money she would save from not having to get a new one. Maybe something very frivolous—a $100 bottle of Shoot the Moon. Or a pair of ostrich-skin cowboy boots for Nina that she would quickly outgrow.

"There's a guy in this support group I go to," Ozzie said, "who said his daughter is addicted to sniffing the gas out of cans of whipped cream."

"Support group," Tuesday said, standing. "How did all my friends get so old and confused?" Ozzie had finished shaving, and Tuesday pulled his Spider-Man mask back down to cover his face. She put her lips to the lips of the mask for a tiny kiss, then turned to leave.

"I tell you what we're going to do," Ozzie said, taking off the mask. "You're going to go home, pack a few suitcases, then we're going to steal our children away before somebody else does it. We can throw the girls in the back of my pickup. We'll drive from town to town, busting church windows at night, repairing them during the day. Then we'll move on."

"That's sweet," Tuesday said, closing the door behind her as she left the bathroom. Walking down the hall, she day-dreamed about a runaway afternoon with Ozzie in a motel room, drinking pink champagne and playing gin, while Charlotte combed out weeks' worth of snarls from Nina's hair.

PART TWO

iiiiiiii
A FEW weeks after the execution of her husband, Nanette
Schrock returned to her house on Plum Street. She'd been living in Lincoln with her aunt for several months, and no one in
town had seen anything of her except on the television news,
briskly climbing courthouse steps, shading her eyes, bumping the shoulders of reporters and ignoring their requests for
comment. Her hair was cut in a severe shag with a fresh drugstore dye job, in a shade called "mink," according to the women
around town, and she always gripped in her gloved hand a
can of Whooptydoo, a grocery-store brand of cola.

A college literature professor who had been conducting po-
etry workshops at the prison had fought for Robbie Schrock's
life in its final days. The professor had had to walk past pick-
eters and protesters calling for the head of the killer, and he
was joined in his efforts by a pair of frail nuns with long jail
records for their years of peaceable, anti-death-penalty
demonstrations. The governor, with shoe-polish-black hair

that resembled the dip and weave of a toupee, presided lazily over a hearing during which the professor read some of Robbie Schrock's poems about God and forgiveness, about wrenching regret, about his boys playing cowboys and Indians with cap guns and slingshots in the clouds of heaven.

The professor wept as he described how Robbie Schrock was teaching himself lullabies on a plastic piccolo, and that was when everyone remembered how they recognized the professor. Only months before he had been on the news defending his selection of a gay man's AIDS memoir for his freshman lit class, a selection that a few of his fundamentalist students were denouncing. *Of course,* people began to realize, *the man is in love.* Some could sympathize; though Robbie was a child killer, he had a full head of curly hair, freckles on his cheeks, and honey-colored eyes. There were a few women in town who joked in hushed tones that they would have happily sacrificed their brats to have such a handsome husband to visit in prison.

Nanette Schrock attended every hearing, saying nothing, seemingly so confident her ex-husband would fry for poisoning her boys that she chewed on a pencil, puzzling over the newspaper's crossword. A victims' advocacy group spoke on Nanette's behalf, and she had provided them with ample ammunition in the fight against her ex-husband's reprieve— the advocacy group's leader, a plump, grandmotherly woman, stood in front of the governor, her old friend. She held up a pair of tiny, fuzzy, footed pajamas patterned with cows leaping over moons, and she read a prayer that one of the boys had written for a Sunday school class. In it the boy asked God to bless Mommy, Daddy, Grammy, Grampy, the president, the wild dog that lived beneath the back church steps, and the little girl in the news who had fallen in a frozen lake and had had to have all her fingers and toes cut off.

A writer for the editorial page of the *Lincoln Journal Star,* a columnist opposing capital punishment, complained of the manipulation in the next day's newspaper, pointing out that the boys would have outgrown the footed pajamas years before. But it was so weak, this writer's argument that the very young boys had not been such babies, that he apologized profusely in the next edition, as did the newspaper's publisher.

The people of Bonnevilla had at first left their scarecrows and jack-o'-lanterns on their porches in the days after their early-September celebration of the execution, seeing no reason to box them up, only to unbox them come October. But when they started noticing that the lights of the house on Plum Street were lit in these encroaching fall evenings that were growing cold, they began to take down their Halloween decorations, worried about their effect on Nanette Schrock. Nanette was suddenly always in her backyard, wearing a wide-brimmed straw hat, cutting away the dried bramble and dead thicket of her neglected garden.

Then, within the first few days of October, Nanette taped in her window a child's drawing of a red-eyed black cat in mid-hiss, its back arched, its hackles raised in the shape of the teeth of a saw. Everyone then returned their Halloween decorations to their trees and eaves and front lawns, taking the child's drawing as a statement from the silent Nanette that she just wanted everything to be normal.

7 .

♦♦♦♦♦

H U D rested his neck on the cracking red leather of the barber's chair, indulging in an old-fashioned professional shave,
complete with a fat stogie smoldering between his fingers that
he couldn't stomach to actually smoke. He'd grown out his
sideburns and would stop in weekly to have Wilson trim
them to a trendy point.

It was early October, and Hud hadn't had a drink since
September 20, a Jack and Pepsi with a maraschino cherry. He
was proud of the ease with which he'd given up the hooch.
He hadn't been a drunk at all, he decided, or he'd be constantly
itching for a shot, wouldn't he?

On September 20, he'd been invited to Steak and Black
Coffee by Tuesday and her family to celebrate Nina's casting
as the lead lemon drop in her dance class recital. He had
wanted to propose a toast but had worried that he would look
even more like an alcoholic if he raised only his glass of cola,
so he allowed himself the shot of whiskey and went home

mostly sober, feeling a buzz only from the moment that Tuesday had kissed him on the cheek to thank him for wearing a necktie. She had then wiped the trace of lipstick away with her thumb.

Beneath the plastic cape covering Hud in the barber's chair, he wore the uniform for his new job—a secondhand tuxedo for playing piano in the lounge of an interstate Ramada Inn. It was a twenty-mile drive every evening to the hotel, and the tips weren't always fantastic, but some nights they were. The hotel entertained conventioneers, and the career women with nametags pinned to their silk blouses would get sauced on mango margaritas, the house specialty, and they'd group at the table next to the piano requesting tunes like "Love on the Rocks" and "Islands in the Stream." Hud would wink and smile, make his voice as smoky as it would go, and he'd unbow his tie and undo a few buttons of the ruffle of his tuxedo shirt. Sometimes he'd sneak in a few of his own songs—"Penny," named after a fictional lover with copper-colored eyes, was particularly popular. The ladies would buy him drinks that lined up, undrunk, across the top of his baby grand.

After paying the barber, Hud stepped outside into the autumn evening, pulling his jacket tighter around him.

A few doors down from the barbershop, in the doorway of the long-defunct Hotel Juliet, stood Charlotte in a trench coat and a polka-dot headscarf. She was bent a little, scratching her calf through a rip in her dark nylon stocking.

"Don't you ever stay home with your daddy?" Hud asked, blowing on the coal of his cigar to spark it back up, then holding it toward Charlotte. She held her hands open over the cigar, warming her palms with the smoke and its puff of heat. "You look like a goddamn hobo," he said. The front of her coat was missing most of its buttons.

"I've been divesting myself of my worldly goods," she said, and at first Hud thought she said *whirly* goods, which he liked the sound of. "All My Whirly Goods" would make a nice song title.

In the crook of her arm was a small pink-and-white-striped paper bag from Victoria's Secret that she used as a purse. She reached into it and took out a few sour-cherry candies, offering one to Hud. As he took the candy, he noticed a red dot drawn on her palm—he'd been seeing these mock stigmata on the wrists and palms of some of the girls around town. One of the girls who gathered on the lawn at the flea market to hear him sing had taken a marker to the hands of her two younger sisters as he performed, and afterward she had made them bow their heads and recite some prayer about wounds and virgins. The other night, as the skinny waitress at the Steak and Black Coffee gave him his change, Hud saw she had red dots on both the front and the back of her left hand.

Hud licked his thumb and grabbed Charlotte's wrist to try to rub the mark away. "Don't, you crazy bastard," Charlotte said, pulling her hand back. "It's taken me days to get it that red."

"There's something wrong with you," Hud sighed. "There's something wrong with all of you. It's not even the color of blood. It's too red."

"It's better than blood," she said. She pressed her fingertip against the dot.

"And you don't even know your stuff," Hud said. "A nail in the palm wouldn't have been enough to keep him stuck to the cross. They would've had to hammer it in his wrist, or he would've slipped right the hell off. Your little stigmata dot needs to be on your wrist."

"A nun in Bolivia named Constance bled from her palms every Thursday and Friday. A stigmatic in Italy bleeds from her shoulders in her sleep." Charlotte walked away from Hud, away from the Hotel Juliet. "My point being: you bleed where you bleed," she called back. The high heels of her yellow shoes clicked noisily against the sidewalk—the shoes had little vinyl bows at their backs, rhinestones at their centers. Even in her castoff clothes, all mortified for Jesus, Charlotte was still the fanciest girl in town, Hud thought.

"Join me for supper," Hud said, flinging the cigar into the street and nodding toward the Waffle Iron, where he often ordered from the breakfast menu at 6 P.M. "I don't know what you're doing out here in the cold night alone, anyway. Your nose is runny already."

Charlotte brushed away his offer of a handkerchief, and she looked forlornly up and down the quiet street as she wiped her nose with the sleeve of her trench. "Junior was supposed to pick me up here. He was going to take me to some church youth group square dance tonight," she said softly, with what seemed to Hud a pathetic pinch of longing in her voice. "Some country chapel near Gothenburg. But sometimes he gets these crippling migraine headaches, and he just has to fall into bed and put a washcloth across his eyes."

"Macho type, eh?" Hud joked, but Charlotte didn't smile. "And I suppose you're madly in love with him."

"Yeah," she said, "sort of, I am."

Hud put his arm in hers and walked her toward the diner on the corner. "Why are you all gussied up anyway?" Charlotte said, plucking some lint from his velveteen lapel. "You're not working the drive-in like that, are you?"

"I quit the drive-in," Hud said. "Word of advice: don't ever work for ex-in-laws." But Red had been good to him since the divorce, too good really, padding every other paycheck with an extra $50 or so and lending Hud his reliable old Caddy a time or two to take Nina to hockey matches in Kearney. The Widow Bosanko would often invite Hud to join her and Red for supper in the office in the back of the concession building. They'd sit around the desk, balancing their plates atop books and stacks of paper, cutting into the T-bones the Widow cooked on the grill behind the projection booth. After eating, they'd all lean back with glasses of thick raspberry wine Red had bottled himself and stare contentedly at the walls papered with faded movie posters. Even as his teeth ached with the sweet of the wine and his stomach still grumbled from the undercooked steak, he felt nostalgic for that very minute, at the very moment he lived it. Hud couldn't bear to think of Tuesday with a new husband, or himself with a new wife, Nina suddenly the stepchild of strangers.

"Oh, take me with you tonight," Charlotte said when Hud told her about his new job. She sat in the booth, removing her headscarf, promising to sit silently in a corner of the lounge drinking baby bellinis. "I'll be utterly peepless."

Hud felt a jolt of pain in his side, some phantom twinge from an old sucker punch to the kidneys. Once, Gatling drove Charlotte to Kansas City on the back of his Vespa for a five-day drunk in a highway motel room. The night the kids left, Ozzie came out to the house calling it a kidnapping, and Hud had stupidly put up his dukes. Hud now touched his ribcage gently through his tuxedo jacket. Gatling's teenaged rebellion had somehow seemed precious to Hud then, and worth defending.

"I'm still recovering from your daddy's wrath of months ago," Hud said. He could just picture it, him taking Charlotte home in the A.M., Oz on the porch with a baseball bat, accusing Hud of getting Charlotte snockered on sugar water to molest her in a ditch.

Hud could always have taken Oz easy, or at least gotten in a jab or two, but he actually thought he was somehow comforting his old friend. The fighting had felt like an intimate exchange, a step toward reconciliation. They hadn't seen much of Ozzie right after Jenny's death, except in a rumpled coat at the grocery store, so it had been good to have him back up and swinging.

The menu for the Waffle Iron was a lit-up contraption at the side of the booth, wired with a red telephone, the offerings unaltered since the 1950s. Hud always ordered the Protein Special, a piece of fatty New York strip with scrambled eggs and a slice of Texas toast buttered to sopping. "Just a bowl of chicken broth for me," Charlotte told Hud as he dialed up the waitress. "With some oyster crackers."

"Christ," Hud muttered, and he ran his finger down the menu. "The lady will have the french toast and a hot chocolate," he said before hanging up as Charlotte complained. "I know, I know," he said. "You're all through with the whirly goods."

Looking across at Charlotte's cheeks, still pink from the wind, Hud thought of his son, and he began to feel weepy. Like some schoolgirl, Hud had once imagined a wedding for the two children, complete with church bells and fat bridesmaids. He pictured Ozzie, handsome as hell in a crappy tuxedo, drunk on bubbly, giving a toast that would bring all the guests to tears as he said worshipful things about Charlotte's dead mother.

"Do you ever think about him?" Hud asked. "About Gatling? Do you ever hear from him?"

"No," she said. She poured sugar into the hot chocolate the waitress brought.

"Here," he said, reaching into the inside pocket of his jacket for the postcard Tuesday had passed on to him about a month before. The picture was of a pink Victorian house with gingerbread woodwork, the sun setting in the ocean in the background. Tiny print at the top of the picture described the house as having been the birthplace of the Rev. Manny Hamlet, famed child evangelist. *We perform on the beach,* Gatling wrote. *Rev. Manny Hamlet even came to one of our shows. He's 94, but everybody around here still calls him the Child Evangelist. He sits in his wheelchair and whispers when he speaks so that the girls have to lean in. He rubbed his thumb against Harmony's nipple. He put his hand on Sunny's hip. I hope I'm someday such a respected dirty old man. xxoo, Gat.*

This was the first, since his conversion, that Gatling had shown even a speck of delight in the sinful. When he first ran away to play guitar for the singing and dancing Daughters of God, he sent Hud and Tuesday magazine clippings with pictures of the band, the four twenty-year-old innocents in elaborate gowns they built themselves on a secondhand electric Singer, according to their publicity. The gowns were white and flouncy, strangely bridal, with bras that pushed their cleavage up and out, but whenever Gatling wrote of Sunny, Harmony, Dolly, and June, he spoke of them as if they were as sexless as nuns. But this postcard suggested that Gatling's life was more than day-and-night piety and restraint. Reading between the lines of the short letter, Hud could sense the beating of Gatling's rebel heart and felt confident that the boy was just inches from entirely defiling that quartet of foolish virgins.

He hoped Charlotte would take the card, would be charmed by Gatling's words, and spend the rest of the night pining for him. But she pushed the postcard away without a glance. "You keep it," she said.

What had happened between Charlotte and Gatling to damage them both? he wondered. Maybe it had been nothing, or close to nothing; all these children were such weaklings. And while a father agonizes about his children done in by things like drugs and liquor and sex without rubbers, along comes religion. Religion, it seemed to Hud, got passed around in town like something infectious. He'd known too many perfectly fine people who, upon falling in love with someone full of faith, quit drinking, quit cussing, suddenly knew nothing but compassion for every living goddamn thing.

8 .

||||||||||
BEFORE stepping into the Ramada Inn lounge, Tuesday checked her lipstick in the mirror of her compact. The curl at her forehead had wilted in the night's light drizzle, so she gave it a twist with her finger to give it more spring. She wouldn't be there at all, she told herself, if she wasn't still buzzing from the most of a bottle of red she had sipped with Oz earlier that evening at the Wiggle Room, a lifeless honky-tonk where the dance floor gave you slivers. Had it not been for the wine, she would never have messed with putting up her hair, with pressing the clingy blue dress that had fallen off its hanger to wrinkle on the closet floor.

"Let me see," Nina said, reaching up for the compact. Tuesday held the mirror before her, and Nina straightened the limp orchid tucked behind her ear. Tuesday had let Nina pluck the flower from the plant near death on the back porch.

"Sophisticated ladies," Tuesday said, snapping the compact shut and swinging her hips, a swing that Nina quickly mimicked. Nina was in her bliss. She had been begging Tuesday for days to take her to hear Hud play piano; Hud had promised a mellow rendition of Opal Lowe's classic country-funk tune, "Snake Eyes and Alligator Shoes." Slowed way down, Hud had explained to Nina, the song's precious melody, and its sentiments about lousy luck and addiction, showed through nicely. Nina had been intrigued.

Inside the lounge, Hud played an Al Green song to a small crowd of lonely zombies. Most everyone sat singly, stirring around their ice cubes with swizzle sticks. The only noise rose from a raucous table of businessmen in mussed comb-overs, the men happy with self-congratulation and stubby cigars.

Nina crawled up into a vinyl seat at the bar, and the bartender gave her a maraschino cherry. "You have ID, little miss?" the woman said.

"This is Nina Smith," Tuesday said, sitting next to her, putting her counterfeit Kate Spade atop the bar. Her sister, Rose, had hosted a purse party during which a representative with rhinestone-studded, dragon-lady fingernails had demonstrated the click and clack of the gilded clasps of a wide selection of designer knockoffs. Tuesday bought the Kate Spade and a Gucci and got slightly soused off the pitcher of fuzzy navels Rose had mixed up.

"Hud's daughter," the woman said with a wink, placing cocktail napkins atop the bar. "I hear you're a little musical too. Maybe we can get you to sit on top of the baby grand later and belt out a few tunes." Nina blushed from the bartender's attention. Then, when the woman said, "You must be Tuesday," Tuesday blushed too.

The woman introduced herself as Augustine, then offered to buy them both a drink. "I make a mean virgin sex-on-the-beach," she said, winking at Nina again.

"She'll have that," Tuesday said, loosening the knot on her scarf. "And I'll have . . . well, y'know what, I'm going to have a martini. A Sapphire martini, on the rocks, very very dry."

"Olives?"

"Um, do you happen to have those little cocktail onions? I'll have three of those."

"And this ant will have a grasshopper," Nina said, flicking the insect that had fallen onto her sleeve from her orchid. Nina had been teaching herself the names of drinks in a bartender's manual she'd found at the flea market.

Hud had apparently noticed their arrival, as he'd begun to play "Scar Baby," a song of his own he'd written about the afternoon he first proclaimed his love to Tuesday, when they were both only seventeen. "You wouldn't love me once you got me naked," she had told him as they creaked down the Platte River in an old rowboat. "I'm covered in horrible scars. My father tried to dissolve me with battery acid when I was a baby." Hud then stripped her teasingly, slowly, lifting an inch of blouse here, pushing down an inch of underwear there, looking for some hint of any kind of scar. All he found, once she was entirely naked, was a white crescent moon next to her belly button, from when she rolled over onto a piece of glass while sunning herself in the backyard when she was fourteen.

"I think I'll order martinis when I'm older," Nina said as Augustine swished some vermouth around in the bottom of a glass before pouring the liquid into the sink. "It comes with something to eat. Does it come with one of those little umbrellas?"

"No," Tuesday said, not looking back at Hud as he sang but feeling as if he stared at her, as if he stood right at her back, his breath on her neck. "You'll have to drink a Singapore sling to get one of those." *Skin milk-white in the moonlight/me counting new scars and old freckles.*

Tuesday took a sip of the gin, hoping to stave off the sobriety she felt creeping up on her tipsiness.

"Go make a request," she told Nina, handing her a dollar. As Hud played the Opal Lowe all slow for her, Nina sat next to him on the bench. Tuesday picked up their drinks and her handbag and scooted into a corner banquette. Hud had kicked off his shoes, working the pedals of the piano in stocking feet. After Nina's request, he dipped into his own collection of original songs, playing some of the more melodic ones—"A Lovely Afternoon for a Crying Jag," "Secondhand Go-Go Boots," "A Broken Heart and Crazy Glue."

He sang about going to New Orleans with Tuesday on their second honeymoon. In the song, Tuesday stands in a street in the French Quarter, shading herself with a $2 umbrella and clutching a paper sack of souvenir voodoo dolls made in Taiwan. *I'm crooning about my voodoo honeymoon,* he sang with a witchy zing, Screamin' Jay Hawkins–like, *my tired bride waiting for a jazz funeral in the hot rain.*

Tuesday thought about how easy they'd had it back when they'd thought everything so impossible. Practically every Saturday night, Hud and Tuesday and Gatling had shown up at Oz and Jenny's back door for what they all considered an evening out. One night in the fall, Charlotte and Gatling, only about six and seven years old and in their pajamas before dark, rolled out their sleeping bags beneath the piano in the sunroom, the coldest room in the house. The adults had cocktails in the brightly lit kitchen, and they indulged Hud as he played a new composition on the plastic strings of Charlotte's toy ukulele. As he strummed out "The Rain Puddle Waltz," Tuesday and Jenny, the only two in the room who knew a proper two-step, danced in the cramped kitchen, giggling, bumping their hips against the stove and fridge and table, tripping along.

Hud announced to the club that he was taking a short break, then picked up Nina from the piano bench to carry her to Tuesday's banquette. "Did I ever tell you," Hud asked Tuesday as he tickled Nina's ribs, "about how this child was born with nothing but bleach-blond fuzz on top of her bald head?"

"I was there when it happened," Tuesday said. Hud wore a potent aftershave, though his chin was stubbly, at least two days this side of seeing the business end of a razor blade. But knowing Hud, the sloppy look—the crooked tie, the stocking feet—was probably calculated. He liked to make women want to baby him. It even still worked on her, and she had been seeing through him for years.

"Your head looked like a peach," Hud said, "so your mommy wanted to call you Georgia. But your pappy wanted to call you Peaches."

Tuesday smiled at this fiction. They had decided on Nina's name hours before they saw her head bristled with peach fuzz; they had named her after Al Hirschfeld's daughter. Tuesday had been enrolled in a correspondence caricature class at the time and, too hot and heavy to move an inch that last summer month of her pregnancy, she spent her hours puzzling over Hirschfeld's drawings in a book, scanning them for the name of his daughter hidden among the scribbles of a can-can dancer's skirts, or in the lines of the brilliantined hair of a movie actor. Lying in bed, a cold rag at her forehead, she'd been pleasantly hypnotized by counting Ninas.

"Can I change my name to Peaches?" Nina said, lying down in the booth, resting her head on Hud's leg, her feet in Tuesday's lap.

"Not until you're older," Hud said. "When you're an emancipated minor."

"A fancy-panted what?" Nina said.

"An eman-ci-pa-ted mi-nor," Hud exaggerated, faking sign language, fluttering his fingers in front of Nina's face. "Somebody call Miracle Ear. This girl needs to schedule a fitting."

"I wish I *was* deaf," Nina said, covering her ears. "Because you talk too much," and Hud tickled her more in retaliation. Tuesday sat idly by, mildly amused, stoking her drunk with her martini refill. This was a familiar role for her: an audience for Hud's little vaudeville act with his children. She had often come across as the sourpuss in the family, sitting at the kitchen table playing solitaire, drinking supermarket sherry, as Hud worked his children into a slaphappy frenzy. Even as the marriage fell apart, Hud remained Nina's comic foil, filling the house with laughter that turned Tuesday gloomy. Because once Nina conked out for the night, Hud would fade away, bored with the notion of simply loving his wife. *You have a man who's madly in love with his children,* Rose had told Tuesday as she had first contemplated divorce. *You're the luckiest idiot I know.*

"Speaking of emancipated minors," Hud said, taking Gatling's postcard from his jacket pocket, "you can have this back." Gatling sometimes sent the postcards to Hud's address, sometimes to Tuesday's, which Tuesday hoped was some sort of nonverbal effort to make his parents visit each other, some gesture of concern. It hurt Tuesday that Gatling never asked after anyone in the family, not even Nina, whom he so adored. Tuesday glanced at the postcard, but then returned it to Hud's pocket. "I want him back, Mother," Hud said. "Let's go on TV and cry our eyes out. Let's say they brainwashed him."

"We were the ones who kicked him out of the house once or twice," Tuesday said. "We sent him away to camps. Facilities. He was giving you gray hairs in your sideburns," and she touched his sideburn. He reached up to take her hand, and she let him hold it for a few seconds before pulling it away.

"Well, then, we'll say that *we* were brainwashed. What, we're the only two goddamn losers in the world who aren't allowed to unmake a mistake?"

"Don't swear in front of Mommy," Nina mumbled, halfway to falling asleep.

"Our Nina, always the pope," Hud said. "We'll do things differently with this one," he said to Tuesday, pointing his thumb at Nina. "We oughta at least make some money off her when we cast her off. Sell her to the circus, or to a carny." He leaned closer to Tuesday. "You smell pretty," he told her.

"No," she said, "my sister smells pretty. She borrowed this scarf and stank it up with her perfume." Tuesday didn't hate the idea of Hud being in love with her again, she had to confess. But wouldn't everything be easier if he just skulked off like a wounded mutt? Wouldn't it almost be better if he was relentlessly bitter, wishing her the worst? "What about Augustine over there?" Tuesday said. "Don't tell me you haven't even asked her out. Don't tell me you haven't even stolen a kiss. She's a beaut. Stunning baby blues. She's very statuesque, I'd say." She found herself leaning toward him as she spoke, her voice low.

"You and me," Hud whispered in her ear. "We'll get a room in the hotel. We'll just sleep, nothing else. We'll keep our clothes on. I'll be good. Nina can sleep in the bed between us." *Pat my head*, Tuesday thought, leaning her head on his shoulder. *Tell me I'm too drunk. Tuck me in like the gentleman you ain't.* "Let's try it out, Day. I don't care what happens. I don't care if you kick me to the side again. Mess me up, if that's what's got to happen, I don't care. All messed up by you is about a hundred times better than nothing."

"Where was all this sweep-me-off-my-feet shit a year ago?" Tuesday said.

"You can't convince me that you're happy," Hud said, his fingers soft at the back of her neck.

"I'm happy as hell," she said. "There are things I definitely don't miss."

"What don't you miss?" He kissed her cheek.

"I don't miss that," she said, "for one thing," as she leaned in for another. "I don't miss those patronizing little kisses whenever I tried to talk seriously about things."

"Then don't let me do it," Hud said, kissing her again. He put two fingers on her chin and brought her lips to his. "Stop me," he said. Tuesday closed her eyes, eased by the familiarity. *A kiss by the catacombs of witches long undead,* Hud had sung in the song about their second honeymoon. Tuesday remembered the tour they took of a cramped New Orleans graveyard with its crumbling mausoleums and stone angels streaked with pollution. As they stood in line to peek through the cracked lid of a marble sepulchre at the skeleton of a dead stranger, Hud whispered in Tuesday's ear, "Don't kiss me."

That was a little thing they had. During some unromantic moment, or moment inappropriate, during a dull church service or in the hallway of the grade school, Hud would whisper, "Don't kiss me," and Tuesday would look around, then swiftly steal a kiss.

As she kissed Hud now, she recalled another honeymoon, a fourth or fifth, to a seaside town in Florida. They were forever leaving their children with the grandparents, escaping in efforts to revive their marriage, declaring any vacation a honeymoon in order to treat themselves to champagne and suites, while the shingles of their house decayed and the termites became legion. Still winter, Tuesday had lain on the beach in long sleeves and long pants as Hud ran the cool, smooth edges of a piece of pink sea glass across her cheek, her throat. Later they walked too far, watching the tide, and had to lean into the strong ocean wind as they walked back, Tuesday's eyes tearing up. The skies were overcast, with just one strip of clear blue, one thin line cut through the clouds like the exhaust trail of a plane. "Don't kiss me," Hud had said when he'd sensed she was angry. And she had been, blaming him for some reason for the cold and the wind, so she hadn't kissed him.

What did I have to be angry about? she thought now. A long walk along the beach? Why hadn't she just kissed him? she wondered. What would it have cost her, that little kiss?

"Get a room," Augustine said, winking, setting down another martini.

"Oh, take it away," Tuesday said, too softly and too late, as Augustine returned to the bar. She remembered she'd been eating onion after onion. "My breath, I suppose," she said, putting her hand to her mouth.

"Nothing wrong with your breath," Hud said. He lifted the glass to hold it to Tuesday's lips. She took a sip, then pushed his hand away. Tuesday had never been much of a drinker before the divorce; she'd even verged on the holier-than-thou about it, trotting off alone to Al-Anon meetings to yack about the bad habits of her husband and teenaged son. She didn't get much comfort from the meetings—she would glaze over from the store-bought crullers and the oversugared Sanka and the hard-luck scenarios that made her own life seem only troubled and not at all wrecked. But she liked writing, "Gone to Al-Anon, Back at 6" in big letters in black marker on a full page of notebook paper she would stick to the fridge with a magnet shaped like a strawberry.

When Hud took a drink of her martini, Tuesday said, "I thought you were on the wagon."

"Well, I don't think I've been on the wagon since I started kissing you five minutes ago," he said, "inhaling all that hooch."

Tuesday knew she was too drunk to do the smart thing. She sat up straight, picked up her phony Kate Spade, clutched it to her chest. She held the scarf to her nose and breathed in the scent of Shoot the Moon. She wished she was more like Rose. Despite being completely unlucky in love and lousy at keeping a job, Rose was always utterly cool. Rose made all the wrong moves with real aplomb.

Tuesday took her keys from her purse. "This is no good," she said. "I shouldn't be out drunk with Nina."

"So stay here," he said, tugging at her keys.

"Yeah, I can just see us," she said, picturing herself and Hud, drunk, x's for eyes, in a hotel room, the bed filled with empties. She picked up Nina, then began to scoot from the banquette. Hud grabbed Nina's ankle, making Nina groan and wake a little.

"Let go," Tuesday said, and Hud did, causing Tuesday to stumble as she stood. Hefting Nina up and out the door was awkward; Nina was too big to be carried these days. *I'm no kind of mother,* Tuesday thought, dreading the next day and the long, sober afternoon. She would spend it in bed with pots of tea, wracked with guilt, worshipping God just long enough to thank him repeatedly for sparing her from some drunken car crash. *I'll start going to church again,* she thought now, already praying and negotiating.

As Hud followed her from the lounge and to her car, he said, "Give me the keys" a few times in what sounded to Tuesday, annoyingly, like a threatening, fatherly tone that he never deigned to use on his own darling children. She shifted Nina in her arms to unlock the back door of the car, then laid her down across the seat. When Tuesday turned to Hud, he took hold of her right hand, gripping hard. Her fist tight in his grip, she felt the keys digging into her skin.

"Give them to me," he said. "I'm not letting you drive drunk with my daughter."

"Oh, I'm not the drunk in this picture," she said, though quite clearly she was. She knew she shouldn't be driving. One more martini and she would have been blind with double vision. There was an old motel just down the highway; she could see, as a speck of green light, its lit sign featuring a girl in a swimsuit poised to dive, advertising the heated pool that had long since been filled in. She would inch down the highway, as slowly as she could, and check in there for the night.

"What happened?" Hud said.

"Hud, you've asked that a million times, and I've answered a million times, and I don't have any more . . . words to . . ."

"No, no," Hud said. "I mean just now. What happened tonight? It was really nice there for a minute or two." He sniffled, either from the cold drizzle of rain or from disappointment. She couldn't quite tell, even looking right into his wet eyes. "And you got all dressed up. And the pretty hairdo."

"Hud," she said, "something like this, whatever this is, you know, it would take time. It took me years to get up the gumption to finally divorce you to begin with. I move slowly." Tuesday leaned back against the car, and the pressure of Hud's grip built. "That hurts," she said.

"Then drop the keys."

"I can't drop them," she said, "until you let go."

"Grow up, Day," Hud said. "Give me the keys."

"*You* grow up." *Why can't you chuckleheads refuse to speak to each other like other parents do?* Gatling scolded one morning when he was fifteen, interrupting some lazy spat of Tuesday and Hud's. *Or just stab each other in the throat, and put us all out of our misery.* Then, miraculously, Gatling wept, his feet up on the kitchen table, as he ate peanut butter from the jar with a steak knife. Tuesday and Hud just sat there, stunned to silence, fumbling with their coffee spoons and Sugar Twin as everyone pretended that Gatling wasn't soaking his dirty t-shirt with tears. Tuesday cried a little then too, embarrassed, but mostly relieved. It had been wonderful to see her son, already at that point out of reach and out at all hours, showing signs that he gave a damn.

"I'm serious," Tuesday said, feeling some pain work up her arm. "Let go."

"Give me the keys then."

Tuesday just looked at Hud, and Hud looked back, the hard pressure of his hand steady. *What was I thinking?* she thought. *There's something so wrong with us.* Then she felt him squeeze just a pinch tighter, but enough to make the pain unendurable. "Fine, have the keys, you psycho," she said, giving him a kick in the ankle, "but you're breaking my freakin' hand." She only meant to be melodramatic when she said it, but when Hud let go, and she felt the weight of the keys, she recognized the pain of fractured bone. In the sixth grade, she'd fallen trying to walk down the basement stairs in roller skates, intending to practice her figure eights on the concrete floor.

"Shit," she said, dropping the keys to the pavement. She tried to close her fist and wiggle her fingers. "Oh, great. Great."

"What?" Hud said.

"I think it *is* broken."

"I didn't break your hand," he said, rolling his eyes, reaching out for her elbow.

Just snapping back her wrist, stepping away from Hud, gave her another jolt of pain. "No, you did. It's like, it feels like funny-bone pain, like when you bump your funny bone, except kind of worse." But maybe it wasn't broken, she thought. Maybe it was only sprained, or just out of joint. *Please, just be out of joint.* "I can't believe this," she said, cradling her wounded hand in the other. Hud tentatively put his fingers to her elbow, and she allowed it.

"Are you . . . are you crying because it hurts, or . . ." Hud said.

"I'm not crying," she said. "It doesn't hurt that bad." She stood there, looking intently at the palm of her hand, searching for the letters of her daughter's name among the crisscross of the hundreds of lines.

"I should take you to the emergency room," he said.

"No. No," she said. She wiped her eyes with the back of her good hand. "I'll go to the doctor's office tomorrow."

"You know that I didn't mean to hurt you, right?" Hud said, gently taking her wrist, tracing his finger softly across her open palm.

"I know," she said. She had to leave without another word or she knew she would end up cradling his head to her chest, pitying him for his clumsiness. But when she bent over to pick up the keys she'd dropped on the pavement, she stumbled and had to grab hold of Hud's leg to steady herself.

Hud squatted next to her, leaning over to whisper in her ear. "I really can't let you drive," he said. "Just stay here at the hotel, please. I won't bother you. You can check in under an assumed name."

"Like what?" she said, letting him kiss her neck.

"Mrs. Smith?" he said.

"I'm already Mrs. Smith," she said. "That'd be a dead giveaway. You'd be on to me in a second."

"Mrs. Jones?"

"OK," she said, standing, "I'm Mrs. Jones." Anxious to get out of the wet and the cold, and to put her aching wrist in a bucket of ice, she walked off, leaving Hud to collect Nina from the backseat. "And I don't want to see you for a while," she said, though she suspected, from the sound of the clop of his boots, that Hud was too far behind to hear her. "There's something wrong with us. We're lousy for each other."

A little later, in a motel room that smelled of a mix of stale cigarette smoke and the pine-tree air fresheners that hung from rearview mirrors in cars, Tuesday sat on the floor next to the credenza to call her sister. As she spoke, she struggled to peel off her pantyhose with only her left hand.

"Maybe I'll get my hand in a cast, and all the kids in my art classes can doodle on it," Tuesday said. "'What happened, Mrs. Smith?' 'Ah, well, you know, I got shit-house on gin, then when I went to drive my daughter home, my ex-husband, who I had been making out with in the bar, broke my hand because I wouldn't sleep with him.' I mean, what kind of white-trash shit is that?"

"I'll come get you," Rose said, yawning.

"No," she said, "I'm too tired to do anything about it tonight."

"If it's a fracture, you could make it worse," Rose said. "By sleeping on it wrong. It could get twisted around. Remember Ann-Margret's toothache."

"Remember Ann-Margret's toothache" was an old family warning from when Rose and Tuesday were little girls visiting their grandmother. Bored on the farm, lazy in the rockstone branches of a fallen tree in the pasture, the girls would drink fresh lemonade so gritty with sugar the sweat bees would hover above their lips, and they'd read their grandmother's Hollywood tabloids. Though mostly scandal and gossip, the papers occasionally featured a story of celebrity ill health. For some reason, one article had haunted the sisters for years: Ann-Margret, or someone like her, had ignored a simple toothache for a few days, resulting in an infection that coursed through her body, provoking a fever that nearly killed her. Over the years, Ann-Margret's toothache had been invoked mostly as a metaphor for leaving things too long unsaid.

"I'm not going to sleep wrong," Tuesday said. "I probably won't sleep at all."

"Well, whatever. Just don't tell Dad that I didn't rush right up to get you. Or I'll be the one in big trouble."

"I don't plan on telling Dad much of anything," Tuesday said. "I'll just say I fell off my roller skates again." Nina, in the room's one double bed, began to snore, exhausted from her perfect evening on her father's piano bench. "I'm so glad that Nina slept through the whole thing."

"Yeah, she's usually such a light sleeper," Rose said. "Are you sure she was asleep, or was she just playing possum?"

"OK, this conversation has ceased to bring me comfort; I'm hanging up."

"Call me if you want me to come get you," Rose said.

When she got off the phone, Tuesday turned on an old movie channel and sat up in the bed, still in her blue dress. She rested her hand, throbbing some, on a pillow in her lap, and with the other she gently rubbed Nina's back. A foreign movie played, black and white, one she didn't recognize; its white subtitles were washed out by the white tablecloth of a scene in a café. An occasional word would reach past the tablecloth and spill onto the black skirt of the woman drinking from a tiny cup. *Place. Red. Lost. Winter.*

Closing her eyes, Tuesday listened, lulled by the French conversation. Her father had worshipped Jean-Paul Belmondo and, while working for a movie distributor, had collected some prints of his films as well as an original poster for *Une Femme Est une Femme,* with Belmondo's signature scrawled just beneath Anna Karina's pout. After Red moved his family to Bonnevilla to buy and refurbish the defunct drive-in, when Tuesday and Rose were teenagers, he would show his favorites on winter nights, the theater closed, the girls wrapped in blankets next to the drafty window of the concession booth that looked out onto the screen. Tuesday would rest her head on Rose's shoulder, swooning from watching the handsome Belmondo through a flurry of snow, the French dialogue crackling on the office's antique speakers.

One Saturday night Rose had even consented to chop Tuesday's hair short, like Jean Seberg's in *Breathless*. It wasn't long after that that she first spoke to Hud at a keg party in somebody's basement. Hud had just had his heart stomped by a girl named Kitty, and he wore a jean jacket she had left behind in his car. This Kitty had bedazzled her name across the front pocket, and the jacket was too tight on him, too short in the sleeves.

"From *À Bout de Souffle*," Tuesday had said, explaining the inspiration for her haircut and using the movie's French title in an effort to sound brilliant and strange. Hud confessed he didn't know the movie, but he sang a few lines from a song he'd written about a French foreign exchange student he had once dated who had worn a wristwatch that ran fast. That night Tuesday sat with him in his car, resting her head against his shoulder, scratching off the sequins spelling out Kitty's name.

Huddling into the sheets of the motel bed, Tuesday imagined the life she might have had, had she not gotten pregnant and married so young. She conjured up a one-room flat in Paris and a meager life of scrimping, working days selling newspapers and peppermints, spending nights painting until morning. The particulars of Tuesday's life fell away as she condensed her belongings to all that would fit in an attic apartment. Falling asleep, she peopled the place with favorite objects—her grandmother's hand-painted teapot on the windowsill, a Japanese lantern over the light bulb, the upright piano she never learned to play, pushed into a corner, leaving just enough room to open the door a crack. She saw herself alone in the room only a little uneasy, only mildly distracted with regret for having never had babies.

♨♨♨♨♨♨♨♨♨♨♨♨♨

9

A U G U S T I N E put her hand in Hud's, telling him to squeeze as hard as he had. She had locked up the lounge, and she and Hud sat together at the bar.

"No," Hud said, still holding her hand, taking a sip of the splash of Jack she had poured for him in a cordial glass. *Just a few gulps to unrattle your nerves,* she had said. "I don't want to put your arm in a sling too."

"I just can't imagine that you broke any bones," she said. "You probably just pinched a nerve in her hand. I'll prove it to you. Squeeze. It won't even hurt."

Hud wanted to. He wanted to squeeze as hard as he could, just so Augustine would continue to sit there smiling, batting her eyelashes, convincing him she didn't feel a damn thing.

He turned her wrist to read her watch. Almost 2:15 A.M. Upstairs, Tuesday was likely fast asleep. Hud considered renting a room across the hall from her, then joining her and Nina in the morning so they could sit around in rented terrycloth robes eating room-service eggs over easy. He would allow Nina to stunt her growth with a cup of coffee just the way she liked it—nearly white with sugar and milk.

"I'll get you some more," Augustine said, picking up the glass.

"Thanks, but no," Hud said. Augustine was usually stingy with the liquor after last round. She had been the one to convince him to give up drinking in the first place, though he'd never believed himself to be half the drunk some of his friends were. But she'd been right in her preaching about how a man of thirty-five, a father of two, should have a certain respectability.

Hud thought of his own father, unbelievably likable, but no one you'd admire. In old Polaroids, Nicky Smith had been handsome in red denim leisure suits and glittery tie clips, in sharp contrast to Hud's stringy-haired mother, who'd had ill-fitting false teeth ever since a teenaged car wreck. Before he'd left his family for another woman, Nicky had had a short-lived business as a photographer, going up in crop dusters to take aerial shots of area farms. He'd then print the pictures and frame them and go door to door, coercing the farmers into buying the blurry, overblown photos of their own property. Most of the farmers, happy to please such a pleasant man, and vain about their houses and fields, bought the photos, but some didn't. Hud, who hadn't seen his father in well over twenty years, had found all the failed sales attempts in a box in an attic after his mother died. Hud had hung them in the sunroom of his house, above the piano, sometimes losing himself in the photos of the roofs of farmhouses somewhere, of fields thickly green with summer, thin creeks sparkling with reflected sun.

Augustine set more whiskey before Hud, as well as an open tin box. At the lip of the box, Augustine's parakeet, Lucinda, perched. Lucinda's wings had been clipped so she could hang out in the lounge without taking flight up into the ceiling fans. Hud whistled at her to make her trill a little.

"She knows over six thousand songs," Augustine said, mocking Hud's claim on his resume. It was a number he'd plucked out of nowhere to get the job, and the powers that be had worked it into the newspaper advertisements for the club along with a photo of Hud looking contemplative and holding an unlit cigar.

Hud wondered if he'd ever do anything at all inspired before the end of his life. Years ago, when newly wed, it hadn't seemed so far-fetched to fantasize about being discovered playing his guitar for the grim happy-hour crowd of the Cocktail Cherry, the bar down the alley between L and M Streets. Talent scouts were supposed to haunt the hopelessly out-of-the-way. Tuesday, who read the gossip rags while working the register at 12th Street Package, had told Hud that people like Sam Shepard and Jessica Lange and Debra Winger and Lisa Marie Presley thought it hip to skulk, unrecognized, in narrow Nebraska dives.

"You want to know what's sick?" Hud asked Augustine. "What's sick is that I may just want Gatling back in order to ruin his life. To keep him close to nowhere, so he can accomplish nothing, just like his dear old dad, and his dear old dad before him. That's probably what I want more than anything."

"You haven't accomplished nothing," she said. "And you love Gatling. You want him back because you want him back."

Augustine put her hand on his arm, and Hud realized he was only flirting now. He thrived on the tender sympathy she offered whenever he fell morose—a hand on his knee here, a peck on the cheek there. Actually, he wanted the best for Gatling; he admired how his son, at seventeen, saw nothing but misdirection when he looked ahead at a life in Bonnevilla. Though Hud hadn't seen Gatling leave, he had an image of his son running away, fleeing his mistakes on his Vespa, his blue guitar strapped to his back. When Hud had been Gatling's age, he'd wasted hours in his bedroom listing the songs that he'd have on his first, second, and third albums, songs he had yet to write or to hear in his head, that existed only as titles—"Marlboro Reds and Pink Lemonade," "The Johnny Cash Blues," "Salty Wounds," "I Knew You When."

A year later Hud was married, Tuesday pregnant. Neither had even been drunk the night they conceived Gatling. The two had been in Hud's bedroom, stunned dumb with true love, a box of rubbers left in the nightstand drawer. Afterward they'd spooned naked, both shivering despite the heat of the room, the sheets kicked to the floor. They'd already started to worry.

Some nights Hud stayed over at Augustine's duplex, her bachelorette pad, as she called it, sparsely furnished with a few zebra-print beanbag chairs and a sofa shaped like a woman's red kiss. Hud would sack out for the night on the cushions of the lower lip.

Augustine got him to down another shot of whiskey at the lounge, and she insisted he was too sleepy for the twenty-mile drive back to Bonnevilla. Hud liked the idea of sticking near the Ramada Inn so he could check on Tuesday in the morning. As he lay alone on Augustine's sofa, his tux in a pile in the middle of the living room floor, he tried to convince himself that Tuesday's hand remained unbroken. He put his own left hand in his right, squeezed, evaluated the pain. What the hell was he supposed to have done? Hud wondered. Let Tuesday drive away drunk, their daughter unbuckled in the backseat? What kind of father would just shut his eyes to such a thing?

"Stop worrying," Augustine said, suddenly there in the room. In the lamplight from the open door of the bedroom, Hud could see Augustine in only pink underwear and a V-neck t-shirt, her makeup scrubbed away, leaving her eyes looking baggy and tired. "Sleep with me tonight," she said.

Hud sat up on the sofa and patted the cushion, gesturing for Augustine to sit. She did, and he leaned toward her, his shoulder against hers, his arms across his naked chest. He wore only his boxers, and the room was a little too cold. "I'm going to tell you why we can't do that," he said. "We work together, for one. But the main thing is that, somewhere along the line, I fell back in love with my ex-wife. And I still hope that, once I . . . you know . . . stop breaking her bones and shit, that . . . you know . . ."

Augustine laughed, pushing her shoulder into him. "I know all that. But I just had in mind a little tussle. Nothing serious. But you're probably right." She stood up, shaking her head, sighing. "I happen to be in love with my ex, too. I'm the one who threw him out, but here I am, a year later, pining away."

Hud wished she wasn't giving up her lazy seduction so easily; he wanted her to talk him into it. He hadn't had sex since July, when he took Tuesday out to toast the finalization of their divorce. They had been leaning slightly toward reconciliation for a few days, and he thought it would be sophisticated and charming to take her to a riverside seafood place for $35 lobster. They got dressed up, and he gave her a gift of a book about famous divorces—Cary Grant and Barbara Hutton's, Liz Taylor and Richard Burton's.

Augustine leaned against the bedroom door. "Tuesday didn't seem so dumb," she said, "but she's just as big a joke as I am. What is it that we're thinking when we think we'll be better off? How do we manage to tell ourselves with a straight face that we can improve our lives? What a big, fat joke."

After Augustine returned to her bedroom, Hud heard her put on some soft music—jangly and foreign with a kind of synth zither sound. Not sleeping with Augustine solved nothing, Hud decided. He would wait for his dick to soften up, then he would go to Augustine's bed—he didn't want to swagger in there with his erection peeking out through the fly of his boxers.

He went into the bathroom and put some Pepsodent on his finger, then ran it over his teeth and tongue. He patted down his rooster tail with some tap water. He'd looked young for his age for years, but that was beginning to change, some acne scars stark on his cheeks and gray stubble in his permanent 5 o'clock shadow. But he liked how he was looking a little bit ragged these days—up until he was fourteen years old or so, people had mistaken him for a girl because of his soft features and long, curly hair.

He used to be as slight as a girl too, and had stressed over the Charles Atlas ads in his comic books that depicted a ninety-eight-pound weakling incapable of defending his girlfriend from a bully. Hud, only twelve, would sit with his copy of *Ghost Rider* open in his lap, afraid that he'd never be able to protect a wife and children. He imagined a world in which stronger men than you lurked around every corner, poised to thieve everything that's yours.

Hud tried to think of all the possible worst-case scenarios, all the repercussions for breaking Tuesday's hand. A restraining order; maybe a change in visitation rights. Tuesday's father would be further disappointed, and Rose would raise her hackles. It was like a flu or a fever, all this worry. Hud would just have to wait for it to ease away on its own.

Hud went to Augustine's room, where she rested against pillows, flipping through a magazine. The room smelled of vanilla from the candles that burned on the windowsill. He sat on the edge of the mattress, his back to Augustine.

"I went to the doctor last spring because of some allergies," he said, "and he told me he'd just been reading an article in a medical journal about some breakthrough inoculation that would allow people to live to be two hundred years old. The science is almost there, he said. But you'd have to be a baby for the inoculation to work. So you and I will be eighty years old, five minutes from death, while these kids have two hundred years ahead of them. When my doctor told me that, I thought, *How shitty.* I thought, *How unfair.* But then I thought about how fearful you'd be, you know, of accidental death. Dying young would be that much more tragic, because instead of losing sixty years, or whatever, you'd lose more than a hundred and sixty. Then I thought, Is that something we should even want? To live to be two hundred? We don't cherish our every day now. We get it into our head that we'll just go on and on and on. Imagine what it'll be like if you think you have some mini-eternity on earth. If you think you'll have all the time in the world to do what you want. You'd never get anything done."

Augustine kissed Hud's neck, touching her fingertips to his spine. "Hopefully it will only be for the rich," she said. "Who wants to be poor for two hundred years?"

Hud's insomnia, usually fueled by too much late-night coffee, sometimes lent itself easily to morbid fantasy. Some nights Nina was the dead one, tempted into a car with lollipops, then left in a ditch with a broken neck. But most often it was Gatling's death he expected to hear described by some stranger on the phone. He could imagine the Daughters of God gone up in smoke after a church bombing, or assassinated while plucking banjos at a prolife rally. And it didn't matter when a night passed without a dreadful word of news, because it could just as well come the next night, or the night after that, or really at any minute of the day. There was no time that a father could reasonably take a breath of relief.

"Ooooh, boy, you're way off someplace else," Augustine said, flopping back on the pillows. She dug a Benson & Hedges from a crumpled pack on the windowsill next to the bed and lit it with the flame from a votive.

"I'm sorry," Hud said. "It's just been a weird night." He lay down beside her, and they passed the cigarette back and forth, both staring at the smoke that rose to the ceiling.

"You shouldn't smoke," he said.

"It's OK," she said. "I drink green tea all day. It has antioxidants."

"Huh?"

"The antioxidants neutralize free radicals. Stops cancer."

"Gotcha," he said. He decided he'd wait for Augustine to finish her cigarette and fall asleep, then he'd go back to the sofa and give some thought to the song coming together in his head. "A Tea Party with Radicals," he might call it, and it might be about how he hadn't kissed any woman other than Tuesday in eighteen years.

But Hud fell asleep before Augustine did, with longing for the suit he hadn't bought from a vintage shop when he was young. It had been a shiny blue-green thing with skinny lapels, very Steve McQueen, and it had been only thirty bucks. For years Hud had regretted not buying it, the suit showing up in some of his songs as a symbol of tawdry dreams lost. It was what he had pictured himself wearing for the cover of his third album, *Late Afternoon on the Moon.*

1 0 .

||||||||

OZZIE, hungover, lay on the concrete floor of his studio drinking yesterday's espresso. He'd spent the early evening before at the Wiggle Room with Tuesday, guzzling the wine they sold for cheap, doing some shots, until she'd left him behind to go listen to Hud play piano.

The church window Oz had broken with a pumpkin days and days before leaned against a wall of the studio, mostly untouched, far from repair. He could barely look at the broken window and all its dizzying biblical allusion. There was much too much of what there should be, all the disparate characters too intimate with each other. Jesus stepped lithely atop a frothy curl of a Red Sea wave freshly parted by Moses. Mary Magdalene, her loose robe revealing an infinitesimal peek of pink nipple, looked to be doing a table dance at the Last Supper.

Though Noah's wife, who had appeared to be adrift not on an ark but on a rib of Jonah's whale, had not been damaged by the pumpkin, Ozzie had delicately broken her away with a small hammer. He took the shard from his pocket now and touched the jagged edge to a cut on his forearm, a cut that started minor from when he knocked a bottle of aftershave into the sink. In the days since breaking Noah's wife from the window, he'd kept his wound fresh, sometimes reopening it and making it bleed a thick drop of dark blood. Oz liked the idea of regressing, his old grief manifesting itself in some new, twisted manner. The act of slicing his skin with Noah's wife felt a private abuse, made him blush with the thought of it, as if with some adolescent sexual shame. He put the cut to his mouth now, tasting, as part of the ritual.

He began to drift off to sleep, still on the hard floor, the room dark with a brewing storm. Oz remembered his wife one spring in a lawn chair, a bird above her jumping from branch to branch on the flowering crabapple, rattling the leaves, sending the blossoms petal by petal to carpet the ground and the lap of Jenny's robe. With a swatter of torn wire mesh, she batted lazily at the fat flies that bobbed and wove above her. It had been during a brief, deceptive spurt of health, when all could convince themselves she still might live. Jenny uncorked a bottle of red peach nectar Oz had brewed himself, and she reclined to reread *Marjorie Morningstar,* a book she had loved as a girl.

Oz woke after only a minute to the sound of silverware jingling against a plate, and to footsteps on the brick walk that wound from the kitchen to the studio. Every morning Charlotte left a breakfast of grapes and French bread and fresh espresso outside Oz's studio door, then skittered away without knocking. Lately, for maybe the last few weeks, she'd been leaving peculiar little gifts on the plate, like a ballerina broken off a music box and a matchbook from a defunct club called the Blithe Spirit on some street in Kansas City. She'd once left him a half-smoked Havana cigar that he smoked the rest of the way while flipping through an antique *Playboy* she had left the day before that.

Oz stood to peek out the window, to watch Charlotte leave the plate, then duck beneath the dried trumpet vine on her way out the back gate.

Her palm up and out to check for raindrops, Charlotte stopped to open an umbrella, baby-blue and see-through, Oz had never noticed before. She wore a new secondhand white denim jacket, a flurry of butterflies appliquéd all up the back. She had taken to accumulating junk again, Oz was pleased to see. He was anxious to go up and snoop in her room, to search for all the signs of life.

Charlotte had been a fat baby but had grown much too thin, Oz worried. As he watched her step into the back alley, he ticked off in his mind all of her frailties.

Oz had spent years assuring himself that most people survived into old age, that the odds of losing Charlotte too were too slim to fret over. Some days he could even convince himself that Jenny's early death guaranteed a long life for his little girl. Because of those lovely odds. Fate, cruelty, even disease, had some decorum. But then darkness would settle in his mind, the cold certainty of disorder reasserting itself.

"It is not ours to question God's intentions," the nearly decrepit minister had intoned at Jenny's funeral, his hands trembling with palsy against the onionskin pages of his Bible. Above him was the stained glass, and the gold-checked pattern of the long blue dress of Noah's wife that Jenny had always admired. "No matter how mysterious, how seemingly heartless, sad, vicious." He practically spat the last word, maybe fed up with comforting the victims of God's childish wrath. Maybe the minister felt he'd grown old enough to scold the Lord.

During the church service for Jenny's funeral, the sun shone just at the other side of the stained-glass window, sending all the confusion of colors to speckle the white of the lilies and the silvery alabaster of the casket closed at the altar.

Why a white box? Oz wondered then, looking away from the altar, away from the lilies. *Why did we choose a white box?* It was the absolutely wrong color, wasn't it? Why a box at all? Oz imagined a fairy-tale burial, preparing Jenny's ruined body himself with perfumes and oils, and rose petals for the bed of her grave beneath a peach tree. He would have gently put her in the ground, just her body in a simple summer dress, her wedding ring on her finger.

Charlotte had sat next to Ozzie in the front pew but rested her head against the breast of Jenny's sister, Ellie. Ellie held her arm around Charlotte, pressing her cheek to the top of Charlotte's head. Oz cleared his throat, sniffled quick, lifted his finger to wipe away a tear with a movement he hoped was inconspicuous. His finger scratched against stubble—no one had even told him to shave, and he hadn't shaved for days. Had he even combed his hair? Oz didn't want Charlotte to know he was crying, but in seconds his body and breath shook with sobbing. He slouched forward, his tears quickly soaking the cuffs of his shirtsleeves. He felt Charlotte's hand on his, but he couldn't look her way.

Oz's weeping grew so loud that even the ancient minister, who'd likely witnessed every conceivable variety of grief, went silent with shock. Oz felt his daughter draw her hand away, and he leaned forward to press his forehead against the wood railing in front of him.

"Scootch," Hud said, having come up the side aisle from somewhere in the back. He knocked his hip against Ozzie, making him make room at the end of the pew. Hud, in a black suit and blue tie, put one arm around Oz's shoulder, pulling Oz up to sit straight, and with his other hand he made a fist that he pounded lightly against Oz's chest. Hud squeezed his shoulder so hard, Oz had a fat bruise for a week. "Cry your eyes out, kiddo," Hud whispered in Oz's ear. Hud whispered some other things too, but Oz couldn't really hear the words; he was comforted nonetheless by the movement of his friend's breath on his ear and his cheek.

Oz opened the studio door and knelt next to the plate of breakfast Charlotte had left him. Before he could even nibble on a corner of toast, he was startled at the sound of a crash behind him. The noise was so loud, he stumbled out the door, his hands covering his head, certain the whole feeble studio was tumbling to the ground. He looked down to see a softball roll out the door and knock over the dented espresso pot. *The church window,* he thought, afraid to look back. But when he did turn around, and he saw the softball had broken only the back studio window facing the alley, he was somewhat disappointed. In the few seconds after the crash, he had pictured the window mercifully beyond repair. He could have claimed to the church board to have been near completion. He could have held the softball up as evidence.

Ozzie heard fast footsteps in the alley, and he ran to the fence. A wood bat had been abandoned to lie on the pavement. Oz looked up and down the alley, seeing no one, then noticed a skinny girl trying to hide behind an even skinnier tree in a neighboring yard. He saw her scraped knee and her laceless basketball sneaker, her boy's tube sock bunched around her ankle.

"Come on out from there," Oz said, trying to conceal the angry shake in his voice. "I'm not mad. You're not in trouble. I just want to give you your ball back, you little asshole." That slipped out, that *little asshole,* and the child, frightened, leapt from behind the tree and sped off. It was Millie, the terrible girl who had spent her summer huffing Freon from people's air conditioners. One of her braided pigtails had unraveled.

Ozzie jumped over his fence and took off after her. But he stopped abruptly when Millie's summer dress caught on a protruding nail at the end of the alley. She frantically but gently tugged at her dress, trying to release herself from the corner of a shed without tearing the light fabric. The dress looked to be brand new, still bright yellow with a pattern of apples still bright red. If she tore it, her mother would be furious. But who was her mother? Who was her father? Millie was ubiquitous about town, but for all he knew, she lived in that ramshackle house in the country all alone.

Ozzie approached Millie, slowly tossing the ball up, then catching it, slick as a schoolyard bully. He had no idea what to do or say, or what exactly he wanted. But it felt like a fatherly instinct, this cornering her and toying with her nerves.

"Did you act alone?" he asked. "Did someone pitch the ball to you? Or did you just throw it up and aim for my window?"

"I was aiming for that dog," Millie said, pointing across the street to a pit bull resting in the grass. The dog had seemed so old even when it was young that its owners had named it Methuseleh. He lay too lethargic to snap at the flies that mistook him for dead and hovered around his snout.

Millie's intentions disturbed Oz but also intrigued him. If only Charlotte's treachery had ever been so simple. Charlotte longed to float from reach, to teach Oz of her irretrievability, while here stood Millie, caught on a nail, dumb and unrepentant, confessing to plots of animal cruelty. Millie's delinquency was an age-old cliché; there were millions of books and pamphlets on how to crush the spirit of a child like her, any number of pills to coax her into a manageable pliancy.

Just as Oz was about to counsel the girl, to ask, *What did you hope to gain from braining a near-dead dog?* Millie loosened herself from the nail and darted around the corner. Though Oz, long-legged, should have been able to outrun her, Millie was wily and seemed to know all the neighborhood's avenues of escape. She ducked through a rip in chain link, crawled beneath the broken picket of a fence. When Oz would stop, bent, puffing, certain he'd lost her, he'd catch a glimpse of her down the street disappearing behind a hedge or rolling beneath a parked car and out the other side.

Oz kept running, but he had lost any interest in grabbing hold of Millie's one pigtail. Millie held no answers of any kind. There was no recompense he could seek from such a wild-haired, undomesticated thing. He kept running because he hadn't run that much, that far, in years.

Oz had mostly forgotten about Millie by the time he'd reached the town square, by the time the clouds had grown blacker and the wind had worked up. He was still running, but others were running too, hurrying to get to their cars as the clouds broke. He could hear the flat brass of the high school band trumpeting and trombone-ing in the gazebo; their sheet music blew across the lawn. The flea-market merchants folded their tables and stands, boxing up their wares. A woman who sold antique Christmas ornaments hurriedly wrapped the blown glass in tissue, the wind knocking a few off her tabletop to the grass.

Tuesday must be here, he thought, when he saw a few children, the first raindrops of the storm smearing their face painting, their little unicorns and daisies dripping down their cheeks. He stopped running, his sides aching, and he forced the softball that he'd held tight in his fist into the pocket of his jacket. He saw Tuesday already across the street, beneath an awning. She wasn't watching the chaos of the flea market but rather looking in through the window of the storefront. As

Oz approached, he saw that, inside, several girls of various heights and sizes spun in amateur pirouettes.

"I thought we all quit smoking years ago," Oz said, holding out his hand for Tuesday's cigarette. He took a drag, then gave it back. "After Jenny died."

"We all quit *everything* when Jenny died," Tuesday said. "Wave at Nina," and Oz did, and Nina waved back, beaming, hopping up and down in her leotard, her short ponytail bouncing. She was all in yellow, with some feathery thing in her hair, looking quite duckish. Ozzie adored Nina, and she seemed to like him—she giggled whenever he tugged on her earlobe and when he called her Swee'pea. But whenever Tuesday and Oz got together, they abandoned Nina to a relative, and they slunk off to someplace out of the way to drink scotch and watch motley strangers try to pick each other up. Sometimes Oz and Tuesday kissed, but they had yet to make it to bed together.

"Let me buy you ladies a breakfast steak at the Waffle Iron," Oz said. "After Nina's little dance lesson. They have a special till noon on Saturdays."

"We're just going to go home," Tuesday said, dropping the cigarette, then rubbing her forehead. Oz longed to follow her back to her house, for the three of them to play Go Fish at the kitchen table as they drank hot chocolate and the rain fell loudly on the roof. This secret fling, or whatever it was, had started only a few weeks before, with Tuesday in a miniskirt, her bare legs goose-bumped, filling the cab of his pickup with soft perfume and nervous laughter, but it was beginning to seem a little dark and a little desperate. After every date, after dropping Tuesday off at her house, Oz went home feeling slightly nauseated from having drunk one too many, and from the bar's smokiness caught in his clothes and in his hair and in the beard he'd been letting grow thick.

Oz was about to suggest that he could get the steaks to go, but suddenly Tuesday held up her right hand from where she'd been hiding it behind her back. She had a plastic cast over it and partway up her forearm. "Last night, when I took Nina to hear Hud at the club, I guess I got . . . well, I *know*, I don't *guess*, I *know* I got a little hammered. And Hud tried to get my keys from me, and I ended up breaking . . . just fracturing, my hand. I went to the doctor early this morning. He said six weeks with this."

"How the hell did you fracture . . ."

"I wouldn't let go of the keys, and Hud squeezed too hard, I guess."

"That piece of shit," Oz muttered, looking up the street, trying to remember where on the square Hud now lived.

"You don't get to defend me, Ozzie," Tuesday said matter-of-factly, crossing her arms, leaning back against the window. As the storm worked up, the fluorescent lights of the dance studio were all that lit the sidewalk where they stood. "The only reason I'm telling you all about it is because I don't want to be secretive and weird, like some battered wife protecting her husband. I'm not an idiot who has a warped perspective on things. I'm as much to blame as Hud is. I mean, more so. I mean, Hud's not to blame at all. And aren't you tired of fighting him anyway? You two have been duking it out since you were fifteen. And Hud can't stand to fight back anymore, because he's heartsick about you."

"Jesus," Oz said. "Sorry." The cigarette on the sidewalk still smoldered, so Oz picked it up, wiped the filter on his jacket, and took another drag. He looked inside to where Nina intently followed the moves of her instructor demonstrating some kind of cha-cha-cha. True, Ozzie and Hud had fought an awful lot over the years, and had often gone months without speaking, but their disappointment in each other had always been brotherly. Even after they both got married and had kids too young, they would get together alone in Hud's basement and have liquor-fueled discussions about the things they suspected they might be missing out on. Oz had thought even then that Hud should be happier with Tuesday. For years Hud's discontent had made Oz want to clock him in the jaw, and from time to time he'd done just that.

"What's he heartsick about?" Oz asked.

"Don't tell me you don't know," Tuesday said, taking the cigarette for a drag, then giving it back. "You don't know that you've been a wreck for years?"

"Not a wreck," Oz said softly. "Not for years." Months ago, when Tuesday's son dated Oz's daughter, Ozzie would sit in his living room alone late at night, jealous of his own child for having a semblance of a life. Some nights he went so far as to keep an alarm clock in his hand for when he nodded off in his easy chair, woozy from his after-dinner nips of whiskey. When he woke he'd go to Hud and Tuesday's house in a sleepy rage. It had calmed him to disrupt their home in the middle of the night, to shove Hud around. He'd loved how Tuesday, usually in a pair of men's pajamas, would gently but firmly demand quiet and order, reminding them all that Nina still slept. Hud, mad, would go back to bed, but Oz and Tuesday would wait up together, drinking decaf and watching a movie.

"I don't have any room to talk," Tuesday said. "I'm probably a wreck these days too. I didn't want to get all depressed at home this morning and just stew in my hangover, so I brought Nina to dance lessons and sat on the square thinking I could do some face painting." She kicked at her little green toolbox at her feet. "But I have to use my left hand, so all these kids ended up with ugly splotches on their faces. They'd look in the mirror, so excited, then, just, this look of horror."

Oz chuckled, taking her good hand in his, running his thumb over her fingers.

"Probably shouldn't hold my hand here," Tuesday said, not pulling her hand away.

"I won't break it," Oz said.

"Very funny," she said, not smiling, still not pulling her hand away. "I don't want Nina to see us like this."

"That's dumb," he said. "Why the hell not?"

"Because, you know, maybe Nina will get upset, and maybe she'll tell Hud, and maybe he'll get upset. Then maybe in the middle of the night some night, he'll just steal her. He'll run away with her. He's threatened to do it. And what has he got to lose, really? Nothing."

"Hud wouldn't do that. Would he?"

"He would love to go MIA. To go underground. Sounds perfect to him, I bet." Tuesday took her hand from Ozzie's. "When you have kids, you have to work at a divorce just like you have to work at a marriage."

"So get back together with him," he said. He mostly meant to taunt, but he did believe Tuesday and Hud had a kind of melancholy love affair that could easily have lasted them into old age, if they'd only bothered to get to know each other better.

The door to the dance studio swung open, with girls and their mothers stepping out into the rain, lifting their jackets up to cover their heads. Oz looked inside and saw that Nina sat on the floor intently fussing with a buckle on her dance shoe. He took Tuesday's face in his hands then and kissed her, and kept kissing her, and she kissed back. Some smart-aleck girl in a pink leotard wolf-whistled as she passed, causing another girl to burst out laughing.

Oz stepped away from Tuesday, winked at her, then ran into the rain. He kept running until he ran out of breath, until his clothes became too sopping wet, his jeans weighing down his legs. He didn't think about anything but getting home and the ache of his muscles. Back in his studio, panting, he peeled off all his clothes as quickly as he could, desperate to feel dry. As he stood there entirely naked, his long, wet hair and beard dripped water down his chest. He suddenly felt the symptoms of a cold cloud his head, so he dug beneath his workbench for a bottle of VSOP he'd gotten one Christmas from an aunt. He started a fire in the wood-burning stove in the corner, tearing out pages of the old *Playboy* and wadding them up for kindling. As a page burned, a model in a bubble bath, with bubblegum-pink skin, sizzled away. The magazine was from the early 1960s, and the woman wore thick eye shadow and a piled-high hairdo and an expression of wholesome delight. There was nothing come-hither about her.

"Life goes so quickly," Ozzie's father had once said in a kindly tone. But the old man was wrong. When you lose something you care about with every bit of your being, every day after feels endless.

Ozzie bent over and took the softball from the pocket of his jacket on the floor. He stood, looking at the stained-glass window, tossing the ball up, then catching it. With the light of the fire flickering in the glass, Oz thought he saw something not quite right among all the biblical goings-on—a little red devil slipping up the skirt of an angel, the tongue of a glowing-eyed serpent lapping at Adam's fig leaf. Sodom and Gomorrah flashed and glittered with a promising and inviting Vegas neon.

The whole beautiful, sinful spectacle, as quick and as practically invisible as it was, made the window almost worth saving. But not quite. Ozzie wound up and pitched the softball. The ball crashed through the glass, hit the back wall, then bounced back to Oz. He picked it up again and threw it at what remained.

You need closure, everyone had said when Jenny died. *Once you find closure, you'll move on.* He had never before wanted any such thing.

11.

ͷͷͷͷͷ

A FEW nights after Tuesday's wrist got cracked, Hud was at the house, picking up Nina for the evening. Tuesday hadn't blamed Hud for what had happened, but she nonetheless made a little spectacle of her injury, wincing whenever she lifted her fractured hand off the pillow in her lap.

Nina decided to wear her kimono in honor of Hud's gift of a boxful of drink parasols he'd snagged for her from the club. On the back of the slick black robe, Tuesday had hand-painted a coiling, red-eyed dragon with several handlebar moustaches. It held a lit firecracker in one of its many fists.

"Go find your shoes," Tuesday said, drinking coffee from a thermos lid.

"In China," Nina told Hud, popping open and closed a puny paper umbrella, "they used to bend babies' feet so they could fit into teensy shoes. People there have feet like dolls," she said, cheerful, as if she thought them lucky.

"And run a comb through that rat nest," Tuesday said, sighing. "Do I have to do all your thinking for you?"

With Nina in her bedroom selecting socks and shoes, Hud said, "Why don't you come with us to the drive-in, Day? It'll be nice. I have the bus, we'll sit on the roof." Ever since Hud's car had given up the ghost on that back highway weeks before, he'd been driving the school bus everywhere, with the bus manager's tentative OK.

"You are not taking that child up on the roof of that bus," Tuesday said, rolling her eyes like she was so bored from her years of correcting him.

"I hate you, Mommy," Nina objected, shouting from down the hall.

"You better hope to God that's not true," Tuesday yelled back. Then she said, quieter, mostly just to Hud with a little laugh, "Because if it is, you've got some long, hard years of misery ahead of you."

Hud snickered and put the stick of a drink parasol between his teeth and chewed on it, like chewing a toothpick. "So let's say we talk about what we're not talking about," he said.

"What aren't we talking about?" she said.

"I think things went real easy-like the other night," Hud said, "up until I broke your hand. We did kiss a little, you know."

"Hud, I was so . . ."

"Yeah, drunk, so drunk, I know. But I wasn't drunk at all."

"Yeah," she said. "And a person might say you took advantage of me."

"Might say that, I guess." They just looked at each other for a few beats, then Tuesday took another sip of her coffee. "And it felt pretty right," he said. "Felt so right that now

I'm feeling inclined to leaning over and kissing you some more."

"Don't kiss me," she said, and she meant it, and Hud thought that was kind of a dirty trick, her taking his old line, *Don't kiss me*, and turning it around on him. But he could tell, from the way she started gnawing nervously on her thumbnail, that she hadn't meant any real harm by saying it. She just simply didn't want to kiss him.

None of these things were his anymore, Hud thought, looking around the room. He touched his fingers to the top of a cigar box on the end table, a box that had held the Churchills he'd handed out at Nina's birth. He closed his eyes, as if divining. "A pocket knife with a picture of Marilyn Monroe in a pink swimsuit and high heels that I bought at a gas station just down the hill from Mount Rushmore," he said. "The glass eye from a teddy bear you had when you were a kid. A snap-on ribbon Nina wore when she was a baby, when her hair was thin. A piece of red string from who knows what." He opened his eyes and smiled at Tuesday, not bothering to check the inside of the box. "Ask me anything," he said, slouching, resting his head against the back of the sofa. "Ask me what's under your bed, why don't you. What's in the hall closet. Looking for something? I'll tell you where it is."

Tuesday cringed as she moved her wrist again, as she turned back to yell, "Nina, hurry up. It'll be dark soon. They're going to start the movie."

"I'm changing again," Nina yelled back.

Tuesday rolled her eyes, then rested her head too against the sofa.

"I'm not going to kiss you," Hud said, "so don't worry. I don't even *want* to kiss you now."

"Hud, I'm sorry, I . . . that I . . . I mean, if I . . . oh, I don't know." She said, pulling at a stitch in a sofa cushion, "I should have my head examined," half under her breath, as if Hud wasn't sitting right there. "What business did I have, for example, getting all dolled up and going to see you play piano? Taking Nina out so late? I don't want us to fall back into something just because it's easier than doing something else. I don't want to ever kiss you again, and I don't ever want to sleep with you anymore. We shouldn't end up back together just because we don't want to be bothered with improving our lives."

"Never another kiss?" Hud asked with a wink, a bluesy tune coming together in his mind, a song he'd call "I Should Have My Head Examined." Though Tuesday was telling him that there was no longer any chance for them, Hud really didn't mind it as a topic of discussion. Talking about how they wouldn't be having sex was somehow sexually satisfying.

Hud and Nina didn't go to the top of the bus, but they did crawl onto the hood, and they looked up at the stars instead of at the movie—one of their favorites, *Your Cheatin' Heart,* with George Hamilton as Hank Williams. Nina, looking like an Eskimo in her hooded parka with its fur trim, lay flat on her back, popping Hot Tamales.

"We're a lot alike, you and me," Nina said, sounding pensive.

"Why do you say that?" Hud asked. Some dried corn-husks from a neighboring field caught a twist of wind and fluttered off like birds.

"Lots of reasons," was all Nina said then.

"Maybe we're Siamese twins separated at birth," Hud said, pushing down his pale blue Foster Grants and looking at Nina over the tops of them. He had put on the sunglasses to look cute for the new concessions girl who had mixed Hud and Nina some hot cocoa. Her name was Dot, and she wore baby-chick-yellow nail polish. Every time Hud saw her, she was holding a wrapped bomb pop to her forehead and complaining of a migraine. "Siamese twins born years apart to different mothers," he said. "Stranger things have happened."

"You ever going to move back in with us?" she said.

"Probably not," Hud said. From his pocket he took the dried bud of a hibiscus bloom he'd picked from a plant on Tuesday's porch, its closed petals as soft as a powdery moth. He opened Nina's fist and placed the bud in her palm. Nina, tiny, seemed barely to ever grow. Gatling had needed bigger clothes constantly; every few months some shirt or pair of pants was packed away practically new. But Nina had been wearing that same parka winter after winter.

"Look," Nina said, tapping at the glass of her mood ring as she closed her fist around the soft bloom, "it's turning green. That means I want you to marry Mom and not Dot."

"I'm not going to marry Dot," Hud said.

"Grandpa says Dot is as mean as a cockfight," Nina said. "Do you ever think about getting a dog?"

"Dogs make me sad," Hud said. "They have sad faces. Even when they're happy to see you, they seem lonely. I don't think they like not being human."

When Nina finally fell asleep, softly snoring, her head on his leg, Hud sat up, his back against the bus's front window, and counted the parked cars—far too few to make the night even nearly profitable for Red. In an El Camino, alone, was Chet Blake, the officer who'd been the one to investigate the murder of the Schrock boys. He'd seen the boys poisoned and blue in their pj's, tucked into their racing-car sheets, on the first morning of November.

Hud began to feel sleepy too, the music of the movie working into his brief dream about him and Nina on a creaking Ferris wheel. When he snapped back awake, his sleepy vision adjusting to the blue tint of his sunglasses, he thought he spotted two watery, weeping figures on the steps of a basement saloon. When Hud squinted, the figures flickered away entirely, the shadows lifting to merge with the haze of cigarette smoke. Though he saw nothing else extraordinary, by the end of the movie Hud had turned the image around and around in his head, determining that he'd seen the figures in Halloween costumes, masks in their hands, their heads bowed in deadly remorse.

PART THREE

⌇⌇⌇

A S word circulated that the Schrock boys, smudgy but clearly miserable, would occasionally flicker across the screen of the Rivoli Sky-Vue during *Your Cheatin' Heart,* people drove in to catch a glimpse of what might be a holy sight. Some brought their binoculars and opera glasses and sat on the hoods of their cars, attentive to every unfocused corner of every frame. They all wanted to be haunted.

By the end of the week business had tripled, and Red took to showing *Your Cheatin' Heart* on a continual loop from dusk until dawn. A reporter for the county newspaper managed to randomly snap a shot of the movie that, once run on pulpy newsprint with its bleeding ink, fueled speculation further—in a scene in the Opry, two tiny specters could almost be deciphered among the shadows of the band.

Hud had no faith in the supernatural, but he expertly orchestrated the whole spectacle, manipulating everything with an ease that inspired him. Maybe there was a profession to be had in designing miracles, he thought. For example, say a slumlord's property is about to be condemned. You simply hire someone to spot a vision, to see the contours of the Virgin in a streak of rust or Christ in a bloodstain on the hallway carpet, call one of the local unethicals at the daily rag, and in days the state diocese gives the dump its seal of authenticity and the slumlord is swimming in donations and offers to buy.

The first night of Hud's sighting, he went to the dinged-up pink Cadillac that old Mrs. Winter had once won for power-selling Mary Kay. Mrs. Winter was a regular at the Rivoli, lonely and long husbandless, and Hud asked her if she had seen what he had seen. Convinced she had, Mrs. Winter was moved to speak of her discovery during her daily community news report on the town's AM radio broadcast.

Later Hud sneaked one of those silk-flower memorial wreaths with a stuffed teddy bear at its center, intended for the decoration of the graves of children, into the dirt at the base of the drive-in movie screen. By Wednesday of that week, a few other wreaths had popped up, but it wasn't until Thursday, when Hud conceived his pièce de résistance, that the shrine really caught on—he sprinkled some candy among the wreaths, seeding the shrine with a couple handfuls of gummy bears, jawbreakers, Cherry Clan, Lemonhead. By Friday, still a few weeks before Halloween, all the stores in town had been nearly depleted of their stock of sweets, and the ground beneath the screen glittered with the foil wrappers of chocolate bars and the cellophane of hard candy.

"A genius gimmick," said Dot, the concession-stand worker with the migraines, who turned out not to be mean at all, despite Nina's report. She was merely sullen, having lost her own little girl in a custody battle. After her divorce Dot had taken up with a drug dealer and gotten sent to the York women's prison for two months; her ex, a successful drywall contractor who had remarried, had snagged a pricey lawyer, and Dot now only had limited visitation rights. But she'd had some intensive rehab and was now clean as a whistle.

"Genius," the Widow Bosanko scoffed. "The whole thing gives me the willies." Hud had once again been invited back into the office for dinner, and they all sat around the desk eating a roasted chicken and some fries made from the sweet potatoes the Widow had dug from her backyard garden. "We're capitalizing on a tragedy," she said, leaning forward to refill everyone's coffee cup. "We should at least not charge at the gate. It's like blood money, really, isn't it?"

Dot began rubbing her temples, another headache apparently tapping at her brain, and Hud, his hand out of sight of Red and the Widow, wormed a finger through the rip at the calf of her fishnet stocking. With his peripheral vision, Hud could see Dot meekly smiling at him. Hud had yet to ask Dot out, but he had stolen a quick kiss a few days before as they both leaned in to examine the insides of the Slush Puppy machine to determine the source of its rattling. Her lips were sticky and sour-appley from the lollipop she'd been licking.

Ever since hearing her story about losing her girl, Hud had felt the little tug of an infatuation developing. He would entertain notions of running off with Dot, the two of them getting hitched in a quickie midnight ceremony. Sometimes, in a certain state of mind, Hud could convince himself that he could live without Nina. He'd imagine a life sunny without Tuesday's moodiness and her back-and-forth affection, without her using Nina as retaliation for whatever she thought he'd ever done that was so terrible.

"It's not as bad as all that," Red said. But for the Widow's benefit, Red acted sheepish, concealing his enthusiasm for the recent upturn in business. Hud knew Red was thrilled to have a captive audience of sorts, to have an opportunity to conduct a citywide cinematic education. He had plans to play, in between showings of *Your Cheatin' Heart*, others from the vast library he'd accumulated from his years of working as a movie distributor on the West Coast—that night he had scheduled *Paris, Texas* and *Rocco and His Brothers*. Tomorrow night he'd sneak in *Mikey and Nicky* and *Pickup on South Street*.

The Widow stopped complaining of bad karma a few days later when the long, deluxe tour bus of the Daughters of God squeezed down the narrow brick streets of the town square. Hud had contacted them via an address he'd found on their website. In a letter (signed only "A Good Citizen") to Sunny, Harmony, Dolly, and June, Hud explained the circumstances surrounding the murder of the Schrock boys. He described the celebration on the night of Robbie Schrock's state execution and the Sunday-night miracle of the boys' appearance on the movie screen. "They were sorrowful there in *Your Cheatin' Heart*," Hud wrote. "We should do what we can to deliver those angels to heaven." He sugared his letter with a Christian zeal, turning the Daughters' own words back on them— he used a line from their song "The Lord's Lovely Lips" about the healing properties of heartfelt music in order to appeal to their vanity and to their sense of obligation as missionaries.

Though the tour bus of the Daughters of God growled loudly on the street just below his bedroom window, the noise of the engine shimmying a teacup of cigarette butts off the sill to shatter on the wood floor, Hud slept through the singers' arrival. He wasn't even allowed a moment of excitement upon seeing the bus, not a second of fast heartbeat in anticipation of putting his arms around his son again—he slept until the Widow called to tell him that the Daughters of God were now parked on the drive-in lot, but Gatling was not among them.

"It seems he's run away from them too," the Widow said.

§§§§§

T H E Saint Ignatius Methodist Church put up the Daughters of God in an old sanctuary of blood-red brick.

"Nobody's supposed to know that's where they're staying," Junior told Charlotte the night after the tour bus pulled into town. "I was sworn to secrecy."

"By who?" Charlotte asked, but Junior didn't answer. They sat on the hood of Junior's car, in a harvested cornfield next to the Rivoli Sky-Vue, waiting for the Daughters of God to take to their makeshift stage near the drive-in's screen. They'd brought binoculars and parked far from the gathering crowd to avoid paying for a ticket, but they could still smell the rancid sweetness thick in the air. An unseasonal heat had spent all afternoon melting the candy that the locals in their pilgrimages had sprinkled in the dead grass of the drive-in.

It wasn't quite dark yet. Junior leaned back against the car's front window as Charlotte assisted with his horror-show makeup. In the basement of the Holy Three Church, the youth group staged a nightly haunted house, every vignette some mean, grisly sermon. Before the guide pulled back each sheet, he'd describe the agony of the person behind the curtain—the suicide among the orange-cellophane flames of hell; the drug abuser pincushioned head to toe with needles and syringes. Ever since the first of October Junior had played the part of an AIDS patient most nights until midnight, the lines and sexy hollows of his face darkened for gauntness, putty applied to his chest and arms for mock flesh-rot.

"Don't you feel like a complete asshole doing that haunted-house thingie?" Charlotte asked. "It's kind of cruel, don't you think? Especially since so many of those church boys are probably gay. Soft voices. Sweet to their moms. Infatuated with Jesus. A bunch of closet cases. But maybe that's what you are. A closet case."

As Charlotte carefully penciled in a pair of crow's feet that spider-legged down the sides of his face, Junior read an unauthorized biography called *The Brides of Jesus: The Divine Maidenhood of the Daughters of God*. He looked up from the book to wink at Charlotte. "You know," he said, "I wouldn't be surprised if I was," then returned to reading.

But Charlotte knew he wasn't remotely gay. The other day one of the youth group girls told Charlotte that she spotted Junior crawling into the backseat of Imagine Baxter's white Olds parked in the alley behind the church. They'd both been still in makeup, Junior riddled with painted-on lesions, Imagine's face whitewashed a bloodless skim-milk blue—in her skit Imagine was a teenager driven mad by the ghost of her aborted baby.

Charlotte shaded Junior's pout with gray lipstick. She freckled his throat with a bruise-colored rouge. Though Junior was on the bony side, he always looked shockingly healthy, his skin a hearty pink.

"I think you're losing a little interest in me, Junior," Charlotte said. At that Junior put down his book and tenderly kissed her throat, then unbuttoned her blouse to kiss her nipple, flicking his tongue pretty expertly for such a goody-good Jesus freak. She was falling completely out of love with Junior, she suspected. She'd spent weeks ridding herself of all the tiniest things—she'd even sold her half-used lipsticks and eye shadows. But lately she'd been haunting the thrift shops again, wasting her money on junk like costume jewelry with chipped rhinestones and party dresses with missing sequins. She'd even permed her hair, though the curls had already gone limp from all the recent rainy days.

"I've heard rumors about you and Imagine Baxter," Charlotte said, only slightly aroused by his running his fingers over the skin of her stomach. She'd been nervous about bringing the rumor up to Junior, for fear he'd readily confess. But Charlotte guessed she needed something dramatic like that to either break them up or set them into that slow, painful start of collapse.

"Imagine's a mess," Junior said. "We've only talked to each other. I've only given the girl a tiny, little bit of advice." He took Charlotte's hand to hold it against his chest. She wondered if this was a trick he'd read about somewhere—make your girl feel your beating heart as you tell her your lies, and she'll believe them more easily. It wasn't entirely ineffective.

"I'm a mess too," Charlotte said, whining in a way she instantly wished she hadn't. "She's not half the mess I am." *I'm falling back in love with Gatling,* she was tempted to say. *How's that for a mess?* But Junior wouldn't care; no one knew where Gatling was. Word had quickly gotten around that Gatling had abandoned the Daughters of God somewhere along the way.

As Junior slipped his fingers into her jeans to touch the lacy waist of her underwear, his easy, smooth, precise moves only made her miss Gatling more. Gatling had never been so graceful with her when they fooled around in the back of the Pontiac Gatling borrowed from Hud. He lumbered around, pinching and bruising her in the process, knocking his teeth against hers when he kissed. He sucked on her tongue too hard, and tried to jimmy himself into her too soon and too fast.

"Why have you stopped asking me to marry you all the time?" Charlotte asked as Junior kissed his way down to her stomach.

"I got tired of fighting your dad," he said. But Charlotte knew that wasn't true. In the last few weeks Ozzie had stopped noticing Junior at all. Had stopped noticing Charlotte, for that matter. In the middle of any night, she could look from her bedroom window to the studio still blazing with fluorescent light. *I could be raped and left for dead,* Charlotte would think, sleepless in a threadbare negligee, brushing her hair, watching her father's shadow stretch and shift across the back lawn. *I could be nabbed and sold into white slavery, and he wouldn't know.* Charlotte would be lulled to sleep with thoughts of all the various ways she could be stolen away and violated.

But even at his most possessive, Oz was little more than a ghost—things would be moved around, there'd be noises, but no one would really be there. Her father was far too weak to save her from herself.

When applause broke out among the crowd, and sharp whistles, Charlotte grabbed the binoculars and stood on the hood of the car. The Daughters of God stepped out on stage wearing short white dresses as clingy as lingerie that shimmered with iridescence. Harnessed to their backs were elaborate wings, fantastical contraptions that flapped to the beat of the music, the girls operating the rigging of their own wings with pull cords on each side. With each flap, feathers fell into the light breeze to flow above the crowd, and everyone raised their arms in hopes of snagging one, jumping up and down, like reaching for a pop fly. Men held their children above their heads, and the boys and girls plucked the feathers from the sky.

The Daughters of God were tarted up in silver stiletto heels, their hair teased into neo-beehives, their lips a slutty wine-red, their eyes shadowed in 1970s blue.

"I was a stranger and you did not invite me in," the girls sang to a disco thumpety-thump that could be heard for miles, flapping the hell out of their wings. "Naked and you did not clothe me/Sick and in prison, and you did not visit me." The song was "Weeping and Gnashing," their first stab at a dance tune.

"Sunny's not with them," Charlotte said. "I hope she's all right."

"This book says Sunny has collapsed on stage eighteen times," Junior said. "She's the bad Daughter of God." He turned the page to a tabloid shot of Sunny in a leather mini and sequined tube top, stumbling from a nightclub.

Looking again through the binoculars, Charlotte followed the path of an errant feather floating away from the crowd, off to the side, rocking slowly to land in the ruffle of Hud's tuxedo shirt. Hud stood there, suited up for his piano-club gig, his bow tie undone, as usual. He didn't seem to notice the feather on his shirt, or anything else going on around him, his hands sunk in his trouser pockets.

Maybe she could buy a sparkly gown, upsweep her hair, and accompany Hud at the lounge. She could slink around the tables as she sang on a cordless mike, running her fingers through old men's toupees for tips. She didn't have much of a voice, but she didn't think she needed one. She and Hud could take their show on the road and seek Gatling together.

Charlotte and Junior stayed through only one costume change—the Daughters of God doffed their wings for hoop-skirted black robes and white tunics that resembled the getups of acolytes. "We dedicate this song to the lost souls of the Schrock boys," Harmony whispered into a microphone. Holding candles, the tiny flames fluttering with their breath, the girls sang of their hearts in anguish. When they got to the part about wanting to fly away from the stormy wind and tempest, they lifted their skirts in unison, and ten or fifteen doves flew out from between their legs, frantically thrashing their wings to rise above the stage and the crowd.

Sunny's absence had been only briefly explained ("She's having shin splints"), but Charlotte had become preoccupied by it, thinking even that she could hear Sunny's missing voice echoing among the others. The Daughters' dance steps seemed slightly off, as if they needed Sunny's feet to keep the kinks from the choreography.

Charlotte drove to the church so that Junior could stay wrapped in a sheet to prevent smudging his body paint. With the Daughters of God performing, the youth group didn't expect much of a crowd, but Junior and his people saw their horror show as a ministry, there to aid every last lost soul who stumbled by. When Charlotte saw the pamphleteers at the door to the basement, waiting for sinners to come up the stairs disturbed and on the verge of being converted, she was tempted to go down herself and touch a matchstick to the papier-mâché stalactites, to torch the whole flammable hell. Though Junior would certainly condemn her for such an act, her father wouldn't. Ozzie would love it if she became a young hellion under house arrest. He'd allow her to devote her whole life to just being his orphan.

But Charlotte got out of Junior's Trans-Am and left the churchyard, stepping through the chill October wind that had returned with nightfall, toward the Saint Ignatius sanctuary. Willow Ave., the street leading to the church where the Daughters of God were rumored to be staying, echoed slightly with electronic noise, the wind tripping the triggers of Halloween decorations. Plastic ghouls bobbed and whimpered in the trees; black cats with glowing green eyes hissed and shrieked. All the amusement fell on an empty street.

Charlotte stepped around to the back of the church, to the tall wood fence surrounding the sanctuary. She hoped to at least catch sight of Sunny at the window, convalescing. Charlotte peeked between the slats and the dried tendrils that still held shriveled deep-red grapes, out onto a yard messy with yellow leaves. Light from an upstairs room rested on a fountain's stone cherub, a little boy mossy with a few broken curls. Charlotte moved along slowly, rubbing warmth into her bare arms, looking for any line in the fence to see through. When she got to the closed gate, her eye met someone else's, and she jumped.

"Who's there?" came a voice.

"I'm Charlotte."

"Not *his* Charlotte?"

"Not whose Charlotte?" Charlotte asked.

"Gatling's," she said.

"Has he talked about me?" Charlotte asked.

"I don't remember him ever really mentioning you," Sunny said. She leaned in closer to the gate, cigarette smoke rising with her words. "But I've run my hands across your name many times."

The previous spring, Easter Sunday afternoon, Gatling called her bawling, distraught over their breakup. She agreed to go to his house to keep him from doing anything drastic, where she found him leaning over the bathroom sink, dripping blood across the porcelain, every last letter of her long first name carved with a penknife into the skin of his chest.

The "c" and the "h" and the "a" and the "r" had been large, but the rest of her name had shrunk letter by letter as the pain of it got the best of him. The last "t" had been left uncrossed, and the ending "e" was just one little line to the left of his nipple. After pouring him a shot of tequila, Charlotte dabbed iodine on his wounds, and she felt foolish for feeling impressed with herself. Though she knew, even as she ran a cotton ball over the lines of damage in his skin, that she couldn't see him anymore, she loved the idea of him going through life with her name forever scarring his flesh.

"Where is he?" Charlotte asked, suddenly Sunny's intimate.

"Last I heard," she said, "he was wandering around Nashville." Sunny leaned into the fence to whisper. "I'd invite you in, Charlotte, but I'm under suicide watch. One of the old church ladies here is supposed to be looking after me. She fell asleep needlepointing. Everybody's worried that if I off myself, too many girls would follow suit. That's something, huh?"

"Do you *want* to kill yourself?" Charlotte whispered.

"No," Sunny said. "No, that's nothing I want to do. But if I did, I'd do it big. I'd do a double flip off the Golden Gate. Or dive under the hooves of a bucking bronco at a rodeo." Sunny chuckled and threw a dry grape up and over the tall gate and it hit the toe of Charlotte's boot. Charlotte plucked it from the ground and stuck it in her pocket to keep as a souvenir of their conversation.

"Sounds terrible," Charlotte said, wistfully, imagining what it might be like to be so beloved as to inspire copycat suicides far and wide. "Can I ask you something?" Charlotte asked. "Why did Gatling quit your band?" She thought back to one 3 A.M., Gatling naked on the end of her bed with his blue guitar, his thumbnail purple-black from a hammer blow from building canvases for his mom. "Please Mister Please," he played, because Charlotte had been on an Olivia Newton-John jag. She'd bought a wobbly turntable at a library fire sale in order to play the records her mother had collected as a child, and she'd coerced Gatling into learning some of the songs she remembered her mother returning the needle to again and again. Even back when her mother had played them, the records had been old and nearly worn out, popping and skipping with every hair-thin scratch.

"He lost his religion a few months in, I think," Sunny said a little cheerfully. "Gatling's a fine one. You must have really twisted him up good to get him to run so far away from you."

"No," Charlotte said, not offended. Gatling had been with the Daughters of God only a handful of months, so all Sunny probably got was the beautifully morose part of the boy, not the useless fits of fever and agony. "I saw him fall apart all the time, about anything," Charlotte said. "Whatever I did to him . . . it wasn't anything special." Gatling had been blessed with the lovingest family she knew, but he just picked at the seams of it.

Charlotte wished Sunny would follow her to her house, where she would describe a life she'd never led. *Here I fell from the steps and had to get five stitches in my broken head,* Charlotte would lie. *Here I threw a fit and kicked a hole in the wall. I tried to hang myself from that chandelier.* She'd describe a girl of fragility and devastating weakness, someone poorly, poorly composed.

14.

♦♦♦♦♦♦♦♦♦♦♦

"**I LOVE** this song," Nina said, beginning some frantic shag to the echoing thump and warble from the distant speakers. Nina and Tuesday stayed far away from the crowd, viewing the Daughters of God through antique opera glasses. Tuesday lowered her gaze to Nina, the opera glasses magnifying Nina's wide china-doll eyes and long, soft lashes, the crooked line of her bangs, a single cheek dimple.

When Nina turned sixteen, Tuesday would escort her to Paris, and maybe Nina would be smart enough to get lost, to disappear into the crunch of a crowd in the Metro and not resurface for years, not until after she'd had some detrimental love affairs and had modeled in the altogether for an artist brilliant and a touch psychotic.

"You feed this girl sugar out of the bag?" Hud said, suddenly there, lifting Nina, making her giggle as he tickled her neck with his lips. He took a seat in a lawn chair across from Tuesday, keeping Nina in his lap, and he asked Tuesday, "What's going on in that cute skull of yours?"

Whatever happened to that? she wanted to say. When they were first in love, Hud would notice Tuesday's every shift of mood. They could be with a group, out, and he'd lean in to say softly, "What's wrong?" before she even realized she was down.

"I was just thinking about what a sour old lady I'll be," Tuesday said. "And how Nina will have to look after me when I can't look after myself. When my wigs droop, she'll be the only one around to give 'em a shot of Aqua Net."

"I'll be too busy being in love with my husband to un-droop your wigs," Nina said. "And I'll have a boy and girl of my own. Gatling and Nina, Jr."

"What kind of name is Gatling, anyway?" Hud said, gruff. "You would think a couple of kids named that child." He gave Tuesday a wink, a half smile, and she remembered an afternoon when she was newly pregnant. She lay in her bed, feeling blue and melodramatic, still in her pj's at 3, plucking the petals from the last of the roses in a quickly wilted winter bouquet. Hud, come down with a cold, read to Tuesday from a beat-up comic book his dad had had as a kid, a Western with a black-hatted cowboy named Gatling. Tuesday was soothed by his low, sickly, scratchy voice, by his boyish sniffle and his cartoon sound effects for the popping of guns and the rumble of horse hooves.

"Are you terribly sad that Gatling's still gone?" Tuesday said, peering again through her opera glasses, focusing on the ice blue of one of Hud's eyes.

"Yes. You're not?"

"I am," she said, though she wasn't, not terribly. She blamed him, though somewhat unfairly, she realized, for her and Hud getting to know each other less and less. Gatling had been a misery from the minute of his difficult birth. And now he was nowhere, it seemed, his postcards only fraudulent evidence—a good life not lived. "Of course I'm sad," she said. "What kind of mother would I be if I wasn't?"

"I've got twenty bucks," Hud said, exaggerating patting at the sewn-shut breast pockets of his tuxedo jacket, doing a goof on a guy looking for a misplaced money clip when it came time to pony up at happy hour. "Draw me. Capture a father's heartbreak."

Tuesday's right hand was still in its cast, and would be for weeks, but she had recently discovered that, with her left, she could doodle distinctive cartoons that somehow resembled her subjects—the shaky lines and oblong circles tumbling together into a twisty fun-house reflection. Before, Tuesday had always struggled with sketching people, arms and legs uneven and noses and eyes unintentionally lopsided. But with just an extra bit of scribble, at twenty bucks a caricature, she had made over $500 from the people who had flocked to the drive-in to line up for the Daughters of God.

"Forget it," she said. "I've just retired. And you might object to my interpretation."

"Just be kind," he said, shrugging. He stretched his leg out to tap the toe of his boot against the side of her transparent pumps. "Because girls in glass slippers shouldn't kick rocks at people."

"They're plastic," she said, lifting her foot to rest it on his knee. He held her heel in his hand and looked at the clear sole—"Seven ninety-eight," he said, reading the price that had been felt-tipped on at the thrift shop.

"Please draw him, Mommy," Nina said. "I want to see what he looks like."

Tuesday took her foot back, then took the charcoal pencil from behind her ear. Performing nights had bagged his eyes, Tuesday thought as she sketched, but she'd always been a patsy for his sleepy demeanor. Late in the day after every late-night drunk, he'd practically whisper each word he spoke. That and his moving slow, and his lazy affection, had seemed like the best tenderness. Sunday nights had been spent on the sofa, the two of them entangled, watching old movies, and sipping some hair of the dog.

"I almost forgot," Hud said, reaching into his pocket. "Hold out your hand, Neen. It's a piece of a bone of a martyr." Nina examined the yellowish chip. A traveling priest, freshly defrocked, peddled the bone chips and the threads of holy garments at spiritual sites across the country; for the last few days he'd set himself up across the road from the drive-in, his van an elaborate mural of a smiling Mexican Jesus, and a Virgen de Guadalupe in hair ribbons, and skeletons dancing in their holes in the ground. Tuesday had bought a 3D picture of a dark, seductive Joan of Arc; by tilting the picture up and back, she could make the flames lick and Joan's full lips part in an expression of pain. In among the Saint Christopher's medals and plastic dashboard virgins and Spanish novenas for sale were some chihuahuas dressed up in neckerchiefs and kept in birdcages. The priest sat outside the van in a tan suit and Panama hat, reading Harold Robbins, next to a sloppily painted sign: DOGS AND ARTIFACTS.

"*Saint Andy was dragged through brambles and thorns in punishment for kicking over a jug of wine in a pagan temple,*"

Hud read from a tiny slip of paper. *"But from his wounds arose a perfume fragrant with apples and honey."*

"You get a haircut?" Tuesday asked.

"Cut it myself," he said.

"Really? Yourself? I'm impressed. It looks like you could have spent seven, eight bucks on it." Hud smiled wide and Tuesday sketched in his lips as a wavy line. She remembered him singing, every Friday night at the tavern, ten years or so before. He had affected a strangled croon in order to sound agonized, and would let a hand-rolled cigarette smolder, unsmoked, in an ashtray on the floor at his feet. A few of the easy songs he'd play with a longneck held between the fingers of his left hand. Tuesday would get dressed up but sit toward the back, ordering manhattans with extra cherries, feigning mystery though everyone in the bar knew she was Hud's wife.

Tuesday had only just stopped wearing her wedding ring the night before. She stuck it in a jewelry box when she went to bed, and dreamt that a bird ate her fingers.

Hud's fingers were ringless too, Tuesday noticed. She added the wedding ring to the drawing anyway, a hard, dark chicken-scratch on a finger of his long left hand. Where *was* his ring? she wondered. Hocked or tucked away? Rumor had it that Hud had been spending time with the trashy concession-booth girl who wore disco-blue shadow on her droopy, come-do-me eyelids. *I'll tell you this much,* Tuesday wanted to tell him now, *I'll suffocate Nina with a pillow before I'll let that druggie start stepmothering my girl.*

"I hear you've been dating," Tuesday said, to stir things up.

"Then your hearing must not be so hot," he said.

"Sure it is," she said. "The gal who works the concession counter. The one whose bra is always showing because she doesn't button her shirt up enough. You know . . . whatever her name is."

"Yeah, I know who you're talking about," Hud said, grinning at Tuesday like he thought he knew her so goddamn inside out. "She's not my girlfriend. And as far as I'm concerned, that's all I've got to say on the subject."

"She has a little girl too, doesn't she?" Tuesday asked, penciling a ukulele into his fist. "I just read in the newspaper about a study. Seems that more people who have daughters get divorced than people who have only sons. Guess we're both a bit hobbled."

Hud covered Nina's ears and cast Tuesday a squint of disapproval. "That comment should resurface nicely in about ten years or so," Hud said, "when she's yacking her brain out to some shrink." Like a coconspirator, Nina sat passively, seemingly happy to not listen, even putting her hands over Hud's at her ears. "I thought this is what you wanted," Hud said.

"What? What did I want?"

"To never kiss me again, is what you said," he said, his voice low. She half wanted him to whisper, exactly that, in her ear. Tuesday knew she could so easily make a mess of everything by breathing just a few immature words. "Come back" or something equally reckless.

"Well, let's not fight about it," she said.

"Fight about what?" Hud said. "We're not fighting."

"Are we not fighting, or are we just not admitting that we're fighting?" she said, adding to the ukulele a curling, snapped string. "Or are we just not talking about the things that'll make us fight?" If there was nothing at all to scrap about, she thought, then why was he so coy about the whole Dot thing, when Rose had most definitely spotted them picking tunes together at the jukebox at the Steak and Black Coffee? They'd played some Merle Haggard, Rose had reported, and Norah Jones doing a Dolly Parton. Hearing about it hadn't bothered Tuesday much, but that had been before she'd seen his wedding ring gone.

Tuesday tore the drawing from her sketchpad. "Read it and weep," she said, handing it over.

"Well, I don't know about you, Nina," Hud said, uncovering Nina's ears, "but I think that may be the handsomest son of a bitch I've ever laid eyes on. If I didn't know better, I'd think your mom had a crush on me, making me look so goddamn drop-dead."

"I just think you can do a little better than Dot, is all," Tuesday said.

Hud sighed and lifted Nina from his lap, sitting her on the ground at his feet. He took a tiny bottle of aspirin from his inside jacket pocket, then popped a few, swallowing without water. "I've *done* better," he said. "Prettier. Smarter. Look where it's got me."

"Look where it's got you?" Tuesday said. She stuck her pencil into the thumbhole of her cast to scratch at some sudden, psychosomatic itch. "It got you to not such a bad place. It got you a beautiful daughter. A beautiful son. A few good years of marriage here and there." She guessed she truly was sad over Gatling's absence, and the fact that he had not shown up with the Daughters of God. Every piece of her broken home could have piled in the car and gone to the diner to treat Gatling to his favorite—a slice of the chocolate meringue, preferably day-old and muddy, the way he loved it back when he was a pretty-faced brat. "What else would you have been doing all these years if you hadn't been spoiling your babies?"

"I know, precious," Hud said. "I was just kind of joking."

Tuesday paused, waiting for Nina to get fully involved in the Daughters of God who'd struck up a dirgelike number. Nina, balancing on one leg, eyes closed, holding the saint's bone chip tight in her fist, did another of her graceless interpretive dances. Watching, Tuesday knew how much she'd hate not having Nina every evening, not hearing her tiny, tuneless voice as she sang along to the most maudlin of country. *Look where it's got me,* she thought.

"I know that it must seem like I never know what I want," Tuesday said softly, leaning forward, "or maybe it seems like I want a lot. I don't know. I just know I want things to get easy between us, for her sake mostly. I want us to have one of those, what do they call them, amicable splits." Hud clucked his tongue, nodded, looked up at the sky, and Tuesday assumed he was thinking of how he could slip "amicable split" into one of his many bitter divorce ballads. "I just want us to be able to talk about things, without anybody getting mad," Tuesday said.

"So you go first," Hud said, leaning forward too. "Spill your guts if you're so gung-ho about being chummy. Seeing somebody new? I know nothing. Because that little girl over there tends to keep her big flap shut too much."

Tuesday could smell the shampoo he'd used for years, some store brand that smelled like sugared strawberries. When Hud had first moved out, Tuesday had used the last of the bottle he'd left in the shower, giving herself some nasty frizz for days. But the scent it left on her pillow had helped her sleep.

"Nobody," Tuesday said. "Just Ozzie, you know, coming around to fix some things. And, you know, we've had a drink or two." Tuesday could have sworn she'd told Hud that Oz had fixed the latch on Nina's bedroom window and had tended to the echoing drip of the bathroom faucet that had kept Tuesday awake for weeks. Surely she'd mentioned Ozzie coming around, if for no other reason than to be wicked, to remind Hud of his negligence in ignoring the house's need for repair.

But Hud leaned back, scowling. He again reached into his jacket pocket and this time took out a closed drink parasol, the stick of which he chewed on with agitation. "Ozzie," Hud said. "The Ozzie who used to come into my very own house, uninvited, and slug me. That Ozzie, you're talking about."

"Of course that Ozzie," Tuesday said.

"So, OK, since we're all chummy here, all amicable, tell me more," Hud said. "You and Oz. You've had a few drinks, a few friendly happy hours or some such. What else?"

What was there to confess? That she and Ozzie got together from time to time to get drunk, and that he got drunk quick, and had a nifty disappearing act a few shots in? Oz, so handsome and tragic, would vanish in plain sight, sitting still but completely gone, as foggy as a phantom.

"I feel like you're getting mad, and I didn't mean for . . ."

"I'm not mad," Hud snapped. He crossed his arms across his chest and spat his parasol off to the side. "So, what is it? You've kissed him? Worse?"

The last time Ozzie had taken her to the Wiggle Room, only a few nights before, she'd sipped a single glass of their lousy screw-top red as Oz had slammed back double bourbon after double bourbon. As she watched discreet lovers two-step slow, she felt such relief from the lack of possibility. Ozzie was lost to all, but that was what she liked about getting sloshed with him, it was what made their kissing so nicely inconsequential. *I had love once,* she thought. *Look where it's got me.*

"Nothing serious is happening," Tuesday told Hud.

"So, what, exactly, isn't happening? Kissing isn't happening? Sex isn't happening?"

"Shhh," Tuesday said, rolling her eyes in Nina's direction.

"I don't think I like the idea of Ozzie being around my daughter," Hud said, standing, shoving his hands in the pockets of his trousers. "My jaw still clicks from when he popped me one just because Gatling had Charlotte out after 10." He leaned in so Tuesday could hear the noise his jaw made when he opened his mouth extra wide. "He's not a reasonable son of a bitch. And look at the shape that miserable Charlotte is in. Before her mom died, that girl was the queen of the spelling bee. She spelled 'loquacious' or some goddamn thing. She played Jane Fonda in a sixth grade production of *Barefoot in the Park.* Now Oz has let her become an out-and-out freak."

"But you've always liked Charlotte."

"I'm just trying to tell you, Day, that I want Nina to have a shot at being happier than the rest of us. I really should just steal her away so she doesn't have to grow up listening to all our dumb back-and-forth." Hud tossed his caricature in her lap. "You might need this portrait to put next to Nina's on the milk cartons. Because what have I got to lose, really? You might want to pencil in some glassy drunk's eyes. Give me some stringy hair, make my teeth crooked. Make sure everybody can see I'm the worst kind of skunk."

"You're so lucky I don't take you seriously," Tuesday said.

Nina had paused in her dance to watch Hud and Tuesday's dustup, her blue crayon once again a mock cigarette between her lips. "Those things'll kill you," Hud said, going to Nina to give her a kiss on the top of her head. He then grabbed a handful of Nina's hair. "Exhibit A," he said, pointing at the crayon. "She's already picking up our bad habits." He then walked away, even his strut a part of his angry song and dance.

Nina shot Tuesday a scarily adult *What's up with him?* look. "He's just crabby because he was hoping to see your brother," Tuesday said.

Nina leaned her head against Tuesday's shoulder and studied the bone chip in her palm. "I want to be a martyr," Nina said.

"Perfect," Tuesday said. "We could use one of those in the family."

ﻭﻭﻭﻭﻭﻭﻭﻭﻭﻭﻭﻭﻭﻭﻭﻭﻭ

A U G U S T I N E ' S mother, who filled in at the lounge on the nights Augustine was off, stood on a ladder to hang a crepe-paper jack-o'-lantern above the bar. In between blending strawberry margaritas for a book club of middle-aged women, Blanche twisted little ghosts from Kleenex and tucked them into the bouquets of ratty silk roses throughout the lounge; she'd dusted off a stuffed witch and propped it on top of Hud's piano.

The members of the book club were intoxicated and for-giving. Some of the ladies had kicked off their shoes and clinked glasses with every new round of cocktails, but they kept their good cheer at a respectable hush as Hud played terribly. They scribbled their requests—Celine Dion and Bacharach songs—on tens and twenties and passed them up. They didn't even seem to mind that Hud kept getting lost midsong, forgetting what he was singing in the middle of a lyric and letting the tune shuffle off, note by note, into silence. The women would applaud when the music stopped, then wait for him to stumble through the next selection.

Hud was distracted by thoughts of Tuesday and Oz alone, perhaps alone at that minute. Hud had let Oz, that bastard, weep all over his best suit the afternoon of Jenny's funeral. Oz had moaned and wailed, making a general spectacle, and Hud had been the only one with the nuts to get up and go to him, to get him to shut the hell up. It should have meant something to Oz, Hud thought, something significant that he had a friend who loved him to pieces and cared about his dignity. Instead, Ozzie vanished, too determined to be inconsolable. Now here he was, the ingrate, horning in on Hud's new ex.

"What's new?" a woman asked, with a twenty for his oversized brandy snifter stuffed with tips.

"Not much," Hud said. His rendition of "Do You Know the Way to San Jose" slipped his mind and left his fingers. "Just doing my little organ-grinder's-monkey routine."

"No," the woman said, giggling in a way she probably thought seductive. "I mean the old song, 'What's New?' Do you know it?"

"Oh, yeah, yeah, I think so," Hud said, giving it a shot. Her request seemed slightly shopworn, her giggle a little rehearsed, as if she dragged out her ol' "What's New?" bit every time she sidled up to a piano man. The woman, whose soda-can curls were piled high atop her head in an outdated mode, lingered there, leaning into the baby grand, tapping her turquoise ring against her rocks glass. Hud knew the words to "What's New?" but he decided not to sing, because he didn't want it to seem that he was singing to her. It wasn't unusual for him to chat up the clientele, but he didn't go in for going all gigolo just for extra tips. "Here for the book club?" he asked.

"No. I'm the concierge at a Sheraton up in Gary, Indiana," she said. "I'm driving to a convention in Denver. To accept an award. Just a little, tiny, nothing award, really. Nothing worth mentioning."

"Have a speech?" Hud asked. He hoped so, so he could ask her to recite it, so he could ignore her and wallow more in his disgust over Tuesday and Oz. He just wanted to sit and stew, to picture them cozy in Hud's house, listening to Hud's dad's jazz records, drinking the last of the booze from the bottoms of the bottles Hud had left behind in a kitchen cabinet.

"No speech," she said. "I'll just wing it. I'll talk about how I worked as a maid for years and years at a broken-down bed and breakfast. And how I had an epiphany while feather-dusting a bowl of glass fruit."

Hud lost his place in "What's New?" so he moved into the middle of "If I Had You," one of his favorites. "I've had an epiphany or two," he said. "Some pretty useless ones. They're difficult to sustain."

"Oh, don't I know it," she said. "When did I ever think that I'd someday be traveling. And in a bar in a silk dress. Getting tipsy on chilled Southern Comfort. About to make a jackass of myself by asking the piano player if I can buy him a drink."

Then "If I Had You" fell apart too, and Hud got caught up thinking about a song of his own he'd been writing, a tune he thought would be perfect for a crooner like Chick Magnum, the pinup boy with the trademark red felt hat. On his album covers, Chick wore Wranglers that looked so tight as to be painful; he sang songs about teddy bears bought in truck-stop gift shops, and babies abandoned in Salvation Army donation bins, and mommies with cancer, and 9/11 widows on Christmas day.

"I'm sorry," Hud said, standing and picking up his brandy snifter of tips. "I'm going to close up shop early tonight. I've had a pretty bad day."

"Just let me buy you one little sip," she said, back to anxiously tapping her ring against her glass. "I'm a good listener, I'm told."

"I wouldn't be good company," Hud said. "I'll tell you what it is. I just found out that my wife is having some kind of something with my oldest friend."

"Your wife," she said. "I didn't see a wedding ring, so I thought . . ."

"No," Hud said, scratching at his bare finger. He'd put the ring in its velvet-lined box the week before, when he'd toyed with the idea of seducing Dot. The night he'd decided to put the ring up, he'd dreamt it had spun off his finger during a raucous rendition of "Jambalaya."

"Actually, she's my ex-wife," Hud said. "And actually, he's my ex-friend. What's *not* ex with me, I guess, huh?" He stuck the snifter in the crook of his arm. "I should give you your tip back."

"Don't be silly," she said. She pulled a business card from her leopard-print pocketbook. "Look me up if you ever get to Gary," she said.

If you ever get to Gary, look me up. He liked the rhythm of that. It would make for a catchy refrain. Two travelers, dressed up for no reason, lonely in a hotel lounge, wedding rings secreted away. *It's raining outside, but the martinis are dry,* or lyrics halfway sophisticated like that. He'd call it "Straight up, Two Olives."

After saying good-night to (a quick peek at the business card) Ms. Eve M. Flannery, Hud slunk from the lounge looking not unlike a gentlemen thief, he thought, when he caught his reflection in the lobby doors, seeing himself with the snifter full of cash, his tux rumpled, his red cowboy boots scuffed away to a shade of pink. He sure did wish he stood up straighter, but he didn't mind imagining himself as a minor outlaw. As he walked to the bus on the other end of the parking lot, he ran his fingers through the bills, estimating. There had to be a good couple hundred in the snifter, he thought. That, along with the small roll of fifties he kept tucked away in a piggy bank, could easily book transport for himself and his daughter to some godforsaken back acre.

Who am I kidding? Hud thought. It killed him to think of Tuesday lonely in the old house, Nina's noise nowhere around. She'd go batty while Hud and Nina, happily on the lam, sunned themselves poolside at some off-the-map motel. *Because Tuesday,* Hud thought, *she's the real weakling of the two of us.*

Nearing the bus, wishing he'd at least kept the caricature Tuesday had drawn, Hud heard footsteps quick behind him. He felt something heavy hit his back, dropping him to his knees, his kneecaps cracking loud against the pavement. The parking lot seemed to buckle and lift beneath him. In the split second before Hud fell forward to hit his cheek on the cement, he thought he could easily get back on his feet and keep the snifter from tumbling from his arms.

Hud remained conscious as the snifter rolled away unbroken, his sense of smell overwhelmingly powerful. Though he was on the ground looking up, he felt like he was above looking down on the man in the parka and ski mask. Hud could smell something chemically evergreen, and cinnamon gum, and the antiseptic burn of the hard liquor the gum was meant to conceal. He could smell stale smoke on the man's parka. In the rush of wind as the man ran off with the snifter full of cash, Hud got a strong whiff of the faint remains of aftershave, a dime-store menthol brand. The culprit, Hud concluded when he caught the hint of baby powder in the air, was a freckled, redheaded housekeeper everybody called Howie; Howie, not much more than a kid, had just fathered a welfare brat.

Then Hud could smell nothing, not the reek of the nearby dumpster nor of the wet leaves at his cheek. And as the pictures in his head floated and shook, he couldn't smell his young father now towering above him, whose breath was thick with the three Jack-and-Cokes he'd drunk at lunch. He couldn't smell the hairspray his mother used to stiffen her 'do, a spray that had always reminded Hud of watermelon and that he had long thought was his mother's perfume. The rubber boots she wore over her dress shoes squeaked as she squatted next to Hud, the back of her hand against his forehead. Hud wasn't ill—he had slipped on the ice as he skidded and playfully spun down the sidewalk pretending to be a hockey player—but checking for a fever was probably the only motherly gesture she could think of at the moment. Hud's mother often seemed so lost in her own thoughts that the outside world could only just barely intrude.

"Well, that's what you get," Hud's father said, "for horsin' around."

But that's what kids do, you cranky son of a bitch, Hud said now, scolding his old man some twenty-five years later. *They horse around and get hurt.* He wished he had faked paralysis as he lay there flat on his back, or had rolled his eyes up, mock comatose, so his father's black heart might have been tricked into skipping a beat.

Hud's father had brought them all along in his truck—he'd had to haul a load of something to somewhere—and they'd stopped in Omaha for some Christmas shopping. The gift Hud had chosen for his mother now sat shattered in the bag at his side, a tea set painted with bumblebees and pansies, though Hud had only ever seen his mother drink Pepsi. Hud had often traveled with his father in those months that he made his living with a dented Peterbilt, shimmied to sleep in the sleeper by the rattle and shake of the truck. Hud sniffed the air, hoping. To this day, he found comfort in the reek of diesel.

Hud woke, his cheek still against the parking-lot pavement. Picking himself up from the ground, he felt like his every bone was popping harshly back into its socket, his entire skeleton slightly askew. Once behind the wheel of the bus, he leaned forward to sniff at the air freshener hanging from the rearview; he could smell nothing, but he was slightly congested from having been out in the cold night air. He drove home, worrying all the way that he might fall asleep at the wheel, wondering if he'd made a mistake in not going to the emergency room. He could at least have wakened Tuesday with a 2 A.M. call from his hospital bed, working her into a fit by telling her not to worry.

He passed the drive-in as its marquee lights went dark. From the highway, he could see the stage still lit, though the Daughters of God had likely long since finished their concert. One of the last cars of the night pulled out in front of Hud from the drive-in's driveway to putt along. Hud didn't pass the car; he was in no hurry to get home and to try to keep from sleeping. He remembered how, a few years before, one of Tuesday's cousins took a capful of over-the-counter cough medicine after having been out doing shots at her own bachelorette party. The girl, nineteen or something ridiculous like that, died in her sleep from the mix.

When the car in front of him slowed down more and pulled onto the shoulder of the highway, Hud was happy that somebody else was up so late and troubled. He pulled along the shoulder too, then walked to the driver's side to tap at the glass. The woman, alone in the car, ignored Hud, her head in her hand as she rubbed her temples. Hud tapped again, and this time startled her. "Do you need a jump?" he shouted, though her engine still purred. What he really wanted was to invite her to the all-night for a bottomless pot of their undrinkable coffee. Maybe she was on the edge of some fascinating state of defeat, and he could talk her through it. But when she rolled down her window, he recognized her, Mrs. Schrock, the woman with the dead kids. The dead *everything*, he realized, seeing her alone in the green light from the speedometer. At one time she'd had a normal life, had had every reason to believe she always would.

"Is your car broken down?" Hud said, not bothering to attempt to reintroduce himself. He'd only known her vaguely, as the woman who'd taken the driver's-license photos at the courthouse, in the years before her tragedy. But Hud was vain enough to be disappointed that she didn't recognize him, since she used to gently flirt with him whenever he renewed. *With that smile you don't seem so innocent,* she'd said once, looking through the lens. *If I was a cop pulling you over, I'd slap on the cuffs.*

"Can I give you a ride?" Hud asked.

Nanette put both her hands on the steering wheel to grip it tightly, and looked straight ahead. "I forgot where I live," she said.

"Oh," Hud said. "Well. You know, maybe I could help . . ."

"It's so funny," she said, interrupting. "My little boy predicted it. My youngest. One day, when they were both pretty little, I was driving us home from the grocery store, and he asked, 'Mommy, what would you do if you forgot how to get home?' And I said, 'Well, I guess you'd have to find our way,' and then he said, 'What if *I* forgot?' And I said, 'Well, then your brother would have to find our way.' Then he said, 'What if *he* forgot?' And I said, 'Then I guess I'd drive around and around until we recognized our house.' But I was wrong, wasn't I? I didn't do that at all. I just stopped."

"I, I, I think," Hud said, stuttering, wracked with guilt for his spiritual fraud. *I'm the one,* he wanted to confess, *the one to conjure your boys out of the blurry backdrops of* Your Cheatin' Heart. Maybe she would forgive him when he explained that it was only an effort to bring his own son home. He and Nanette Schrock could be friends, he thought. They could commiserate. *A child who loses a parent is called an orphan,* Hud wanted to tell her, quoting from an earnest psychologist on a talk show, a grief counselor with a big black bow at the back of her head. *A wife who loses a husband is a widow.* "Where's our word, Mrs. Schrock?" Hud said, so tired he could barely stand. His eyes blinked rapidly with the effort of staying open.

"Those weren't my boys," she said. She put on a pair of sunglasses despite the pitch dark of the unlit highway ahead. "In the movie. I don't know who those children were, but they weren't my boys." Then, "2212 Plum Street," she said, just above her breath, gasping with remembrance. She inched the car forward, seeming to forget that Hud stood there. "2212 Plum Street, 2212 Plum Street," she quietly recited.

I didn't wake up, he thought for a moment, just dizzy enough to think he was wandering around in some dumb purgatory. *Why didn't I just have a drink with Eve M. Flannery of Gary, Indiana?* She probably would've let him talk about himself for hours, he thought. Then Howie and his welfare brat wouldn't be sitting at home, blood on their hands, lighting their fatso stogies with his tip money.

It wasn't until Hud was back in his apartment, standing in the light of his open refrigerator, holding a bottle of beer to the pain at the back of his neck, that he noticed the damage to his tuxedo. His trousers were bloody at the knees and the lapel of his jacket was ripped and hung flapped over. The suit had long been on its last legs anyway, he realized as he stripped down to his boxers. His clothes and boots strewn across the kitchen floor, Hud still worried about drifting off into a fatal sleep.

Hud seemed to remember a snazzy sports coat of reddish-orange velour, with a Western cut, that had been among his father's suits. Hud's dad, upon taking the job of selling aerial photos to area farmers, had invested in a new wardrobe. Hud remembered spending all of one day in the executive dressing room of Rushmore Winslow's, a spiffy men's store once on the town square; an old clerk in shirtsleeves had fussed and tape-measured. "Soak it all in, pipsqueak," Hud's father said, watching himself in the full-length mirror unwrapping the flashy silver foil from a peppermint. "A quality shop like this is on its way to dinosaur. When *you* finally go to buy a suit, Susie Q, you won't get treated like a goddamn king." (Hud's father sometimes called him Susie Q on account of his head of girlish gold curls.) "All these bastards will be long dead, god rest their souls. No offense, Patschky." The old man, on his knees, muttered something unintelligible, his lips puckered around straight pins as he tucked up the trouser cuffs. "Stroke the sleeve of that topcoat, son," Hud's father said, gesturing to the long green coat draped across the back of a leather wing chair. "That's what 10 percent cashmere feels like, case you were wondering."

Rushmore Winslow himself, dandruff snowy against his gently hunched back, brought Hud's father a cup of strong coffee in a tiny china cup. Though Hud's dad's check turned out to be rubber, leading to Old Man Winslow turning un-gentlemanly ("Little boy, you tell your dad," he said on the phone once, "that unless he pays for that apparel, I know a guy who'll ram him so hard that he'll never stop shitting crooked"), and though his father was fired from the sales job within a year, those suits always represented to Hud the zenith of elegance.

When his mother died, Hud found the suits, still zipped into their gold-colored vinyl bags, at the back of her closet; Hud's father had taken little with him when he abandoned them for another family. The suits now hung on an exposed pipe in the basement of Tuesday's house.

Hud poured himself a cup of coffee, stirred in some slightly soured milk and several heaping spoonfuls of sugar, then went to the phone in his bedroom. He punched in his old number with some indignation, certain Tuesday would sleep through its ringing, would be oblivious to the possibility of dire emergency. She had never even bothered to replace the answering machine that had recently quit working. "I could be the police, Sleepyhead," Hud whispered into the receiver, counting the rings, *eight, nine, ten.* "I could have abducted Nina again. There could have been a chase, and I could have driven the bus off a bridge. Wake up, Mrs. Smith, you need to identify the remains of your family. Time to wake up and get the bejesus scared out of you." He whistled. "Yoo-hoo."

After about the sixteenth ring, Nina answered. Hud said, "What are you doing up, for God's sake?"

"I'm *not* up," she said. "I'm halfway not awake."

"Where's your mother?" Hud asked. "No, let me guess. She's out like a light, snoring her life away, while you wander around the house, getting into the household poisons. Or while you open the door to strangers. Am I right?"

"I'm about two seconds away from popping you one," Nina said, yawning. "And not softly either. Hard."

"Honestly. Who talks to their father that way?" Hud asked. "I'll tell you who talks to their father that way: dirty orphans who grow up in the street."

"Dirty orphans," Nina repeated, chuckling. "I put my bone chip in my locket."

"Which one?"

"The saint's bone chip."

"No, dummy, I mean which locket."

"Oh, the one that came with the little doll in it that had pink hair that smelled like dog."

Even in the months before Nina was born, Hud had been buying her jewelry. Nina had delicate silver and gold necklaces, and adjustable rings with precious stones and mother of pearl, but most often she dripped with the fifty-cent pieces of junk—the plastic ruby clip-on earrings, the diamonds that blinked in different colors—sold in the checkout aisles of the grocery store.

"I'm falling asleep," Nina said. "I'm hanging up."

"No, no, wait," Hud said. "Hey, kid, try to remember to tell your mom something for me in the morning. Tell her I need those suits of my dad's. I wrecked my tux."

Hud pressed at the pain at the back of his neck, wincing. He remembered the splotchy line of black-and-blue up and down his back from when he had fallen on the sidewalk that day years before when he'd horsed around on the ice. His father moved out before Hud's bruises faded; he threw his shaving kit and a deck of cards into the sleeper of his semi a few days before Christmas and made a beeline for his new love, a wheelchair-bound woman in Iowa who sold Bibles over the phone and had three girls. Hud's dad had first taken up with the woman on the CB radio, having intense evangelical dialogue over one of the lesser-used channels. Hud had learned all the details in an unrepentant letter of explanation, riddled with Bible verses, his father sent a few months later.

Hud's father had even left behind the Christmas gifts Hud and his mother had bought for him and had put beneath the tree. When Hud emptied the house after his mother died years later, he found the gifts, still wrapped and ribboned, on a shelf in a utility closet, and he stood there, ripping into them—a Norelco and some aftershave in a bottle shaped like a mallard and a novelty necktie hand-painted with a pinup girl in a miniskirted Santa suit. For a second Hud had pitied the kid he'd been, remembering how he'd chosen the aftershave and the sexy necktie because he'd always thought of his dad as more of a bachelor uncle, a slim, sophisticated ladies' man who listened to scratchy jazz records and joked about how he was always a sucker for a funny brunette and a well-shook gin martini. *My children will never be strangers to me,* Hud had vowed right then, Nina still only an infant and Gatling still a boy, as he slapped some of his dad's abandoned aftershave onto his cheeks.

"Neen, can I ask you a question? And will you promise not to tell your mom that I asked?"

"Mommy says I'm not supposed to keep secrets."

"No, no, no," Hud said, "no, she means if somebody molests you or something, and tells you not to tell, that's the kind of secret she means. So this isn't really a secret, don't think of it as a secret, just think, y'know, it's me and you just flapping our gums about nothing she needs to know about."

"Whatever."

"So, I just wanted to ask, is Ozzie there?"

"No," Nina said with a convincing tone of confusion.

"Does he ever spend the night?"

"No," she said.

Hud kept silent for several seconds, thinking if he shut up for a bit, she'd break if she was fibbing. "Did your mom tell you not to tell me if Oz stays over? Because that's a secret too, you know. If you don't tell me, you're keeping a secret, and you're not supposed to keep secrets."

"I'm on the kitchen floor now," Nina said. "That's how tired I am."

"Do you like Ozzie?" Hud asked.

"Yeah," she said. "He's nice. Do you like him?"

"I'm not particularly fond of him at this point in time," Hud said. "But the poor guy's had a string of really, really lousy luck; he probably shouldn't be expected to ever do the right thing."

"Mmm-hmmm," Nina mumbled.

"You're falling asleep on me, Neen."

"Call me tomorrow, Daddy."

"OK," Hud said. "Oh, and don't forget to tell your mom to leave the back door unlocked so I can pick up those suits. But if you can figure out some way to tell her that without telling her that I called in the middle of the night, that'd be fantastic-o."

"Good-bye, Daddy. I love you."

"Sweetie, I love you and I love you and I love you. Did you hear that?"

"Yes."

"So you'll never be able to say that your father never told you that he loved you, will you? Because I'm telling you that I love you," he said, but Nina had already hung up. It didn't matter; she'd eased his delirium.

ⵜⵜⵜⵜⵜ

E V E N as he picked up the brats on his crack-of-dawn bus
route, Hud wondered drowsily, punchy from downing a
thermos-full of coffee, if he'd died in his sleep. What would
they put in, and what would they leave out, of his obituary? *A
man who falsely claimed to know six thousand songs was found
in his bed, having bought the farm, as stripped as the day he
clawed his way out into the world.* "He was going nowhere fast
for years," *said his unsympathetic ex-ball-and-chain.* "Guess he
finally got there, poor bastard."

"You're ten minutes late, Hud," said Millie, the girl Hud
most longed to send through the front window of the bus
with a sudden stomp of the brakes. "What I got on my two
little toothpicks is as flimsy as nothing." She pinched at the
hot pink tights, giving the snug material a sassy snap.

A few minutes after settling into the front seat directly behind Hud, Millie said, "This is what I'm going as on Halloween." He looked in the rearview to see that she'd already

dismantled the sandwich from her lunchbox—she'd chewed two eyeholes and a mouth into a slice of bologna and draped it across her face like a mask. "Tell me that you love it, poopsie-woopsie, or I scream 'rape.'"

"Christ," Hud said, gnawing faster on the licorice whip that dangled from his lips and coiled in his lap. "You're twelve years old. The things that come out of you people's mouths." She stuck out her tongue through the mouth hole and buzzed him a raspberry, then peeled the bologna from her face. Looking at Millie's reflection in the rearview, at her chronic freckles and high forehead, Hud realized there was nothing exceptional about her wickedness. Millie dressed every morning as if three sheets to the wind. Her pink tights, her gingham skirt, her bright-orange down vest—it was the pure ugly of her that nagged at him. Meanwhile, he had no idea what kind of cute duds Nina had selected for herself that morning.

Waiting at the end of a weedy lane was a girl named Belinda, her face a raw pink from psoriasis, her eyes blood-shot from too little sleep. Belinda was everything Millie was not—mousy, pleasant, plump, and she always took a seat at the far back of the bus to read preachy, religious versions of Archie comics—the ones where Betty and Veronica never wore bikinis.

Posted in the middle of the fallow field of Belinda's family's farm was a peeling billboard, an ancient and vague antiabortion message with fading pastel butterflies, not quite visible to the interstate traffic that rumbled through the farmland a mile away.

"Every life is precious," Millie said, reading its message aloud.

"Don't be so naïve," Hud said.

A few minutes after stepping on, Belinda returned to the front. "Mr. Smith?" Belinda said, tapping Hud so softly on the shoulder he didn't feel it at first. "There's a girl in the back. I poked at her, but I think she might be dead."

Excited by the possibility of something tragic, Millie stood on her seat and shrieked. "Oh, no, there better not be nothin' dead on this bus," Millie practically sang. "I better not get traumatized by this."

I could power-staple steak to Millie's flesh, then toss her in with a pack of junkyard dogs, Hud thought as he slowed the bus to a stop in the middle of the dirt road.

The sun was only just up, and the bus still mostly empty. Millie, Belinda, and the two others—a white-haired boy and his teenaged sister, who wore beaded fringe and too much blush—followed Hud to the back. Hud saw that someone lay on the seat, her feet in the aisle, little dirty red bows atop her beat-up dressy shoes, but he doubted Belinda's forensics. He even thought he could hear the corpse snoring.

The feet belonged to Charlotte, as it turned out, the girl fast asleep, cigarette butts on the floor around her, her trench coat open to reveal only a satiny red slip with old torn lace that had turned brownish. She must have snuck in during the early morning hours, while the bus sat blocking the alley behind Hud's apartment.

Hud bent over to pick up the cigarette butts. For the first time since getting clocked on the back of the head the night before, Hud caught a scent—he could smell the booze that had spilled from a bumpy bottle shaped like grapes, and he felt a rush of relief, his nerves settling.

"Why don't you guys all go up front," Hud said, and even Millie obeyed without a peep. Charlotte, looking a bit demented with dried blood on her chapped lips, her hair flyaway with static, seemed to disturb the children more than if she'd turned out to be a stiff.

Hud took Charlotte's hand in his. "Yoo-hoo," he whispered.

"Where am I?" she said, waking tranquilly.

"Good question," Hud said. He picked up the bottle from the floor.

"That shit's treacherous," she said. "It's homemade. One of the church ladies brewed it and gave it to Daddy to knock him out after Mom died. It's been sitting in a cupboard all this time, working itself into a frenzy." She sat up, took a compact from her coat pocket, and flipped up its mirror. She flinched at her reflection, then licked her fingertips to try to smooth down her mussed hair. "I've run away from home," she said. "Not that anybody would notice."

"You're not going to get far in the back of my bus," Hud said.

"That's where you're wrong," she said. She crossed her legs and reached down to straighten the bow on her shoe. "You're going to kidnap me. Leave these monsters in the ditch there, and let's take off."

"I can't think of a worse idea," he said, sitting in the seat across from her. He picked up a toy pistol one of the kids had forgotten, and he popped a few shots in the air. He deeply inhaled the burnt smell of the spent cap.

"We're going to go find Gatling," Charlotte said. "He's in Nashville."

"Gatling's not in Nashville," Hud said, though he had no idea where along the road the Daughters of God had abandoned his boy. He'd snuck backstage to get a message to one of the Daughters as she'd stood in a stark-white choir robe, a roadie plucking her towering platinum wig from her head with one hand, powder-puffing her sweaty cheeks with the other. The girl was practically naked before Hud, wearing only underwear with elaborate belts and trusses, her breasts and butt cleverly hoisted and cantilevered. Hud stammered something about looking for his son, but before he could finish a sentence, a bouncer a full head taller than Hud grabbed him by the neck. "I got half a mind to yank out your peepers, ya perv," the bouncer said before literally kicking him through a curtain back into the crowd.

"I tried to find out where he was," Hud told Charlotte, "but the Daughters of God wouldn't let me get a word in. They wouldn't even accept the song I wrote for them." Hud patted the pocket of his torn tuxedo jacket, which he'd grabbed from the kitchen floor on his rush to the bus that morning. Inside was still the notepaper on which he'd composed a ditty with a few lines that sounded Bible-ish—about lambs and lilies and glossolalia, a word he'd learned from the defrocked priest who'd sold him the saint's bone chip.

"I happened to meet the bad Daughter of God," Charlotte said. "Have you ever just run into someone famous? It's like that chill you get when you almost step on a snake, but in a good way."

Hud was trying to imagine Gatling on the streets of Nashville. He felt a mix of pride and disgust. He loved picturing Gatling toiling around the town peddling his precious little tunes about tragically pretty girls. Gatling's voice wasn't much, but it was tense in a sexy way, and he had just the right look for an alternative-country album cover—filthy blue jeans hanging off his skinny hips, obscenely big belt buckles commemorating old rodeo championships, secondhand t-shirts with peeling iron-ons. Top it off with that silly, shoe-polish-black Elvis Lives hairdo and you've got yourself a phenomenon, Hud thought. Gatling could be the champion heartthrob of a cable talent show Hud occasionally watched on a lonely Saturday night, a contest for country-music hopefuls who perform their do-it-yourself songs for a panel of has-beens in the industry. *But,* Hud thought, *wouldn't it have been nice if I could've just up and left when I was so wet behind the ears, back when nothing frightened the hell out of me?* Instead he'd been saddled with the responsibility of trying not to be as shitty a father as his own had been.

Charlotte said, "Sunny said Gatling was headed for Nashville, last she knew. And she said he'd been religious, but then lost it. Lost his religion." She yawned, then lay back again, getting dreamy. "So I propose to go save his soul."

Hud's first instinct was to get all fatherly on her, to remind her that she was only sixteen years old and too young to be preoccupied with anyone's lousy soul but her own. But all summer he'd thought she might marry the Jesus freak and be folded into a lunatic congregation. She'd become one of those snaggle-toothed country wives who ended up in the news after doing something like dangling her firstborn into a pit of sacred rattlers.

"You and Gatling both could afford to fall a little," Hud said, relieved to hear that Gatling had given up on being born again. *You need to put the fear of God in him,* Tuesday's father had said when Gatling had his first semi-serious brush with the law. At thirteen Gatling had snuck behind the drugstore counter to thieve a *Hustler,* a pack of Sen-Sen, some cherry pipe tobacco, and a box of luxury sheepskin rubbers; only a year later he got sauced on a bottle of grocery-store Beaujolais and drove the Nova of his then-girlfriend (an older woman at seventeen) into an ice machine outside a gas station. Red foot the bill to send Gatling to a Christian camp for hopeless cases, and the boy returned after a month having turned almost deliriously good and madly in love with the Lord; but he also seemed embarrassed by Hud and Tuesday, who often overslept on the weekends and preferred their own ritual of long, leisurely breakfasts of waffles and omelets and the Sunday funnies. Hud secretly hoped for the devil to inch up into Gatling just a bit—and when Tuesday found a freshly rolled joint in the back pocket of Gatling's black churchgoing pants a few months after the Christian retreat, she and Hud celebrated by getting naked in their bedroom and smoking it while listening to a Jackie Gleason record Tuesday had just picked up for a nickel at a garage sale.

Gatling didn't have another bout with religion until just before he left, after Charlotte decided to no longer be his girl.

He'd tried to convince everyone that cutting her name into the skin of his chest was a kind of holy mortification.

"Don't you eat?" Hud asked Charlotte, noticing the bump of her ribs in the thin slip. He whistled toward the front of the bus. "Millie, bring me your lunch." Hud gave Millie five bucks, then put the tin pail on Charlotte's knees. The other children had wandered back too, and they all stared at Charlotte as she devoured the buttered bread that had once held bologna, and as she scooped chocolate pudding onto her finger and into her mouth. She tore into Millie's bag of gummy bears.

"Here," Millie said, taking the wilting cloth rose from the front of her dress and safety-pinning it to the lapel of Charlotte's trench. The pale boy's sister scooted in to sit on the other side of Charlotte, a plastic comb in her hand. She licked the teeth, then went to work on the tangles of Charlotte's hair.

Getting kidnapped would be the best thing that could happen to her, Hud thought as he watched Charlotte dig for the raisins at the bottom of a tiny box. All Ozzie's moping made his home a mausoleum. A neglectful daddy like Oz should be locked up, he thought, no matter what the man's dismal circumstances. But no, if Hud were to simply rescue the girl, buy her a dress and a steak, then drive her to Nashville to keep her from hitchhiking and getting meat-cleavered by a trucker gone psycho, Hud would be the one fingerprinted and mugshot.

Sitting in the seat across from Charlotte, Hud pressed his cheek to the cold window and looked out across the field. The four strapping sons of Vance Maxwell slogged their way toward the bus, apparently tired of waiting. One of the boys practiced his tuba and his marching-band goosestep. And coming down the road was Hilary Meek, the next stop on his route, on a pair of stiletto heels too old for her. *There's no escaping them,* he thought. Even when stopped in the middle of a desolate road, Hud drew every miserable wretch of a child to him, like a backward Pied Piper.

iiiiiiii

I G O T *frisky in Frisco,* a mermaid declared in a dialogue balloon on the front of an illustrated postcard. She sunned herself, bare-chested and red-nippled, on the rocks of Alcatraz. In the week since he'd received the card, Hud had read and reread the writing on the back, comforted by his son's sloppy penmanship. But it wasn't until the evening after Charlotte's talk of Nashville, as Hud sat at his kitchen table conducting an amateur handwriting analysis, discerning a tendency toward rage in the severe slant of Gatling's *Jesus loves you* and a pronounced homesickness in the loops of his *God bless all,* that he noticed the postcard's curious postmark.

The card had not been mailed from San Francisco, nor from Nashville, but from Hot Springs, South Dakota, a small spa town just on the other side of the state line. Hud then checked the postmark of another card he'd recently received from his son, one with a picture of a row of Las Vegas slots spinning lemons and cherries. Gatling's latest stories about life with the Daughters of God, his musical ministry in cities of sin, were pieces of fiction conjured practically under Hud's nose—a measly four hours north.

Though late for his piano gig, Hud stuck the postcard in his back pocket, slapped on some aftershave, and headed off to Tuesday's to stitch together that amicable split they had discussed.

"Hey, darlin', I'm just sorry as hell," Hud rehearsed in his head as he stopped at the corner grocery store to grab a fistful of half-price, half-wilted daisies. Tonight he needed desperately to be welcomed into the house he'd often been kicked out of, to sit, have a cigarette, be poured a shot from a squat bottle of scotch. Hud dreaded returning to the Ramada Inn lounge. He'd never been bullied as a child—he'd been scrawny, so he'd affected a delinquent's squint on the playground that scared people off—but the thought of crossing paths with the punk who had stolen his tips gave Hud a kid's case of butterflies.

Red's yellow Cadillac stretched across most of Tuesday's driveway, with Rose's bug crammed in behind it, nipping at the Caddy's bumper. Hud parked the school bus across the street, then crept across the lawn to peep through the dining room window. *Rose's birthday,* he remembered when he saw what remained of a white cake on a plate, a few candles still burning and dripping their wax onto the frosting. Rose leaned forward to light a slim, ladylike cigar from one of the candles, while Tuesday did a Kentucky foxtrot with her father at the back of the room. Charlotte sat tearing a paper napkin to confetti in her lap, looking defeated despite her effort to gussy herself up—a spot of lipstick, a bent bobby pin.

Ozzie stood at the table's end to uncork a bottle of wine with the manner and ease of the man of the house. Criminal, Hud thought, that Ozzie could be at all comfortable in a place he'd so many nights disrupted.

Hud stepped close enough to the window for his breath to fog the glass. Suddenly Nina was on the other side, having snuck away from the table unnoticed. She breathed on the same spot of windowpane, then wrote "i c u" in the fog.

Hud winked, put his finger to his lips, and moved away to the back door. In the darkness of the screened-in back porch, depressed about not being invited to Rose's fling, he sat at the piano to quietly tap out a few bars of "Do Not Fold, Spindle, or Mutilate," Opal Lowe's suicide ballad that Nina liked to sing in the tub.

Hud stood to open the lid of the piano bench, where Tuesday kept much sentimental junk among the sheet music, then plucked from it a dried white rosebud from an old please-forgive-me bouquet. He put it behind his ear. From a yellowing envelope, he sprinkled some lost baby teeth into the palm of his hand and stuck them in his shirt pocket. Hud then took from the bench a tiny, undrunk bottle of mini-bar cognac saved from a night in a casino hotel suite he and Tuesday had won in a radio trivia contest. ("Patsy Cline's daughter has a name that might give you a cavity," the morning DJ had announced, then asked, "What is it?" Hud had been the first to phone in with "Julie Fudge.") Hud now twisted off the bottle's lid and downed the liquor, psyching himself up to storm into the dining room and wet-blanket the whole merry shebang.

From the bench, Hud took the first pack of cigarettes Tuesday had ever confiscated from Gatling, when the boy was only twelve, some soft-pack Marlboro reds she'd kept all these years.

"Hey, Ozzie, switch the record to something with some kick," Hud heard Rose say, though they were listening to Dinah Washington's perfectly kicky "Me and My Gin."

As Hud lit a stale cigarette, he heard Ozzie bump into the record player, knocking the needle to screech across the vinyl. With only a few puffs, the dried-up tobacco and cigarette paper burnt down to the filter, filling Hud's lungs with a ghastly black smoke that choked him.

He hacked as he stumbled down the hall, into the dining room, past the domestic bliss of the birthday party, and right up to Oz. He grabbed Ozzie's shoulders and shoved him into the china cabinet where the record player was awkwardly propped, sending the needle skipping forward into the middle of a maddening bossa nova. "If you're going to play my dad's old LPs on a shitty thrift-store turntable, at least show respect," Hud said through teeth still clenched on the cigarette's filter.

"Aw, sugar," Rose said, her cloud of eau de cologne thick in the air, "let's not have conniptions on my birthday." Hud had always cherished Rose, and just feeling the soft weight of her hand on his shoulder, hearing "sugar" on her tongue, almost compelled him to turn away from Ozzie. But it annoyed Hud how Oz stood so still, his arms limp at his sides, looking as polite as a door-to-door Mormon in his white shirt and black tie, as if he believed his lack of fight somehow made him the better man.

Hud spat the filter aside. "Don't pity me, you pathetic son of a bitch," Hud whispered, his lips just inches from Ozzie's ear. "You're worse off than I am, don't forget it." Hud gave Oz another shove against the cabinet, and the record skipped ahead into "Come Rain or Come Shine," and a few teacups tumbled forward to bust on the floor.

Oz had no business being at all confident or keeping company with another man's wife. Hud inched his hands back to touch the jut of Ozzie's shoulder blades, and he concentrated on his old friend's freak-show skinniness. It would never be a fair fight, Hud knew. Ozzie, and his lost little girl, were a tabloid tragedy in the works. You'd read about them someday, father and daughter, starved away to *Guinness Book* levels of invisibility.

Tuesday knelt on the floor, collecting the shattered pieces of teacup, clucking her tongue as if they'd ever owned anything other than mismatched china bought for nickels and dimes at this and that garage sale. "Go home, Hud," Tuesday said, tugging on his pant leg with her fractured hand, "or I'll call the police."

Rose said, "Oh, for God's sake, Day." She had poured some whiskey into a wine glass, which she now held up for Hud to see. She swirled the liquor around in the glass, letting it catch and release some sparkle of light in the dim room. "Nobody's inviting the cops over. Here, Hud, drink this. Drink more. Get drunk. A girl doesn't turn thirty-eight every day, you know."

The cognac and the dry smoke still burned in Hud's throat, so he shook his head at Rose's whiskey, trying to think of something mature and profound-sounding to mutter about the lack of comfort in hooch and cigarettes. Maybe he only drank and smoked because he liked the props, holding a glass by its stem, a bottle by its neck. He loved the cold, sharp snap of the lid of his steel lighter, and rubbing his thumb over the lighter's scratched decal of a Vargas girl in a slinky baby-doll. He hoped to grow up to be one of those men who could enjoy a proper happy hour, who took ease from the routine of one martini, then dinner, then TV, then sleep.

Hud unhanded Ozzie and took a step back to straighten the knot of Oz's necktie. Oz had wise, wide-open, gray-blue eyes that had always made him look old when he was young but would probably make him look young when he was old. "You're the rottenest dad around, kid," Hud said, tapping a finger at Ozzie's rib cage. He leaned in to whisper again. "Get to know your little girl a little better," he said, "or she'll run off. She'll be hitchhiking, blowing truck drivers, just to get as far away from you as she can."

At that Ozzie put his hand to Hud's chest to forcefully, but calmly and slowly, push him away. The blowing-truck-drivers bit was likely what finally provoked him, and even Hud realized it was a cheap shot. Hud knew he had no business dragging Charlotte, angelic enough and a long way from resorting to sucking off truckers, into his redneck effort to aggravate her father.

But instead of punching, Oz again acted the gentleman, stepping aside, taking Rose's glass of whiskey for only one sip.

"Who am I, anyway?" Hud mumbled, turning to look at the others in the room. They all feigned distraction, as if they hadn't even noticed he'd stopped their party. The Widow Bosanko brushed some crumbs off the tabletop. Rose swayed to music, though the music had ended. When he looked at Charlotte and saw her chewing, childlike, on the ends of her hair, he nearly apologized to her.

Hud took a candy letter from Charlotte's plate, the "s" from Rose's name on the cake, and ate it while admiring Nina. Nina stood on her chair wearing a dress not only too old for her, but *way* too old for her; with its leopard print and mangy fur collar and cuffs, she looked to be dressed like a hot-to-trot retiree. But Nina, a downright funny girl, somehow pulled it off.

"I'm sorry, have we met?" Hud said, winking at Nina. She giggled, then reached down to scratch at the back of her knee, bagging her loose tights in the process. The itch was quick, but enough to remind Hud of the spider bites she'd shown him the other day. She'd run her finger over the few small bumps on her leg and ankle as if they were something to be proud of. The girl had venom in her skin, Hud thought, because Tuesday never bothered to dust away cobwebs.

At the thought of spiders in Nina's sheets, their fangs in her leg, he reached out and grabbed his daughter around the waist with one arm, picking her up as she kicked for balance. Before he'd even stolen out of the room with her, everyone had begun yelping. Barreling toward the front door, Nina held in his arms awkwardly (his one hand at her hip, his other at her neck), he saw the reflection in the front picture window of the entire party in pursuit: Red rapping his ankle on the ottoman, the Widow sloshing her cocktail, Rose knocking over a floor lamp and sending clumsy shadows rushing across the walls.

Hud made it to his school bus even before the others had stumbled down the porch steps, but it was Nina who slowed his easy getaway. She had begun to whimper as he set her gently on the seat. "Aw, Neen," he said, with a tone of disappointment he hoped she didn't notice. Then he said, "I didn't hurt you, did I, Petunia?" Though her lips trembled, she squeaked out a "Nuh-uh," then, "My name's not Petunia." He pressed his thumb to a tear on her cheek. He considered, for a split second, that it might not be too late to undo the last rash few minutes. He could come out of the bus, swaggering and winking, dangling Nina by the ankle. *It's just a teensy-weensy party prank, you cranky sons of bitches! I'm the birthday clown!* The evening could still end pleasantly, couldn't it? With everyone gathered around the piano as Hud pounded out a polka with ribald lyrics?

But as Tuesday approached the bus, Hud's desire to punish returned, and he gave Nina a quick kiss on the top of her head, then got behind the wheel and closed the door. The old bus, not built for escape, putt-putted, backfiring, inching away from the curb. Tuesday kept pace alongside, pounding at the bus with both her hands. The thought of it—his wife desperate at the door as he ran off with their weeping little girl—gave him a sharp pain at his temples, a pain that worked down to tighten his stomach.

He braked and opened the door. Tuesday stood there in the street, in the flashing red light of the bus's stop sign.

"Don't beat the vehicle with your broken hand, dummy," he said. "You're just going to jack your fist up more, and guess what poor bastard you're going to blame it on." Tuesday's eyes were wet, her breathing hard from the running. She put one foot on the step up. "Look at the postmark," he said, handing her the San Francisco postcard. "Gatling's got to be in South Dakota," Hud said. "We can get there by, I don't know, just past midnight."

Hud wasn't sure if it was Gatling's proximity that lured Tuesday into the bus or the sound of Nina's crying, but he didn't ask and she didn't say. As Tuesday sat behind him to cradle their daughter in her arms, Hud simply closed the door and drove off, leaving the birthday party spoiled on the lawn.

PART FOUR

"**NASHVILLE,**" Charlotte uttered, with a sigh, after having been silent all evening. Everyone lingered on Tuesday's front lawn, looking off into the dark in the direction of the bus's disappearance. Oz undid his tie, his hands still jittery from the evening's confrontation. The Widow dug the muddled fruit from the bottom of her old-fashioned and chewed at the pulp of an orange slice. Rose fussed with the clasp on her wristwatch as Red's comb-over collapsed and fluttered in the gusts of a winterlike wind that had picked up.

"That's where they've gone, maybe," Charlotte told Oz. "That's where Gatling is, in Nashville." Speaking Gatling's name seemed to drop her deeper into her romantic funk. She fingered through her long string of flapperesque plastic pearls like she was counting off prayers on a rosary. Since when had Gatling been back on Charlotte's mind? Oz wondered. Wasn't it only days ago that she'd given away every dumb little gift Gatling had ever given her?

"I thought you thought Gatling was, you know, a little cuckoo for Cocoa Puffs," Oz said. "He cut your name into his skin, for God's sake."

"Right above his heart," she said, her lips in a pout, as she ran her fingers over the skin of her chest. She snapped out of her daze long enough to say, in a whisper of accusation, "Are you in love with Hud's wife?"

"Do you mean, Am I in love with Hud's *ex*-wife?" he said.

Charlotte sighed, then mumbled, "Why do we even bother?" She turned to go back into the house.

When it became apparent that the bus would not be immediately returning, Tuesday's family began to leave the yard, abandoning their initial plans to raise a toast at the strike of 11:53 (the exact minute in the night that Rose had been born back in nineteen-sixty-whatever). Ozzie volunteered to stay and clean up, and the Widow handed him her highball on her way to the Cadillac. Then Rose walked over and took the highball to get at the smashed maraschino among the ice cubes. "Sorry you got all roughed around tonight," she told Ozzie, chewing on the cherry as she handed the glass back. "My entire family is just out-and-out toxic," she said. "We should be avoided at all possible costs." The way she said it, with a wink and a foxy smile, it was clear to Oz there wasn't a speck of regret to her apology. Rose adored her family's failings and its civilized hostility to outsiders.

Ozzie returned to the dining room, where Charlotte sat eating from a puddle of melted ice cream with a soupspoon.

"What if I said yes?" Ozzie asked, though he wasn't in love with Tuesday; he didn't think so, anyway. All he knew for sure was that he loved how being with Tuesday felt both covert and perfectly logical. Back when both of them were married, he used to flirt with her—or he thought he was flirting (a wink, an aside half-whispered in her ear), but it was possible she never noticed. He and Tuesday, when alone now, rarely reminisced about the days before Jenny died, even though, some nights, old times were all he wanted to talk about.

"What if you said yes?" Charlotte said. "To what?"

"To what you just asked me out there. What if I said, Yes, I'm in love with Tuesday?"

"What if *I* said, You're answering a question with a question and that that's not a very good answer?" This time Oz was the one to sigh and shrug. He drank the dregs of the spice tea at the bottom of a cup.

"I'm embarrassed," Oz said. He put on another of Hud's dad's old albums, a scratched Peggy Lee so familiar that he knew exactly on which verse the record skipped—whenever he heard "Is That All There Is?" in his head, he heard the bump in the music too. Hud had been wrong in at least one regard: Ozzie did treat the records with respect. Hearing a song he hadn't heard in years could rush Oz back and settle him gently among the hundreds of simple evenings he'd spent in this very house, when they'd play round after round of card games they taught themselves from the Book of Hoyle. When Charlotte was little, in the years before Nina, the only girly toys Tuesday had for her was a blue buggy from her own childhood, containing a plastic doll bald from having had all its hair loved off. Oz could remember Charlotte clutching the doll to her chest as she lay in Jenny's arms, Jenny somehow, all at once, rocking Lottie, winning at cards, and sipping her white zin without spilling.

"Hud seems to think I don't know my own girl," Oz said.

"Do you want the honest-to-God truth?" Charlotte asked.

"No," he said, then he chuckled, as if he was only joking. "No, go ahead. What is it?"

"I slept in Hud's school bus last night," she said, her voice almost sing-song. It was the same voice she'd used only weeks before to taunt him with hints of her sordid religious awakenings. "Then when he found me this morning I begged him to kidnap me. I tried to talk him into taking me to Nashville. Doesn't that scare the living daylights out of you, Ozzie?"

"Yes," Oz said, but actually what he felt was a complicated relief. Thank Jesus that Hud was such a good man deep down. There'd actually been something reassuring about the evening's dustup, a camaraderie with his old friend that Oz had desperately missed. "And since when have you called me Ozzie?"

"Only for, like, the last, I don't know, two years," Charlotte said. Suddenly, for a second that was breathtaking, Charlotte sounded like the newly motherless 13-year-old she'd been, her soft voice breaking with an inarticulate and fragile anger. "In case you haven't noticed," she said, "I have terrible habits."

"Your mother would have done so much better with you," Ozzie said. He was thinking of Jenny's easy demeanor, how impossible it had been to discourage her. By the time Jenny turned 32, she'd had short-lived careers as a piano instructor, arts-and-craft director at a nursing home, a jewelry store clerk, and a librarian's assistant. "You'd been better off," Oz said, "if I'd been the one to . . . you know. And she'd been the one to . . ."

"What does any of that matter?" Charlotte said, raising her voice and hitting her fist against the table, rattling the spoon on the plate. "You just say things like that to get sympathy. I'm supposed to feel sorry for you because *you* feel bad for making *me* feel bad?" She took a cigarette from a pack left atop the table. Ozzie's instinct was not to nag her for lighting up in front of him, but to egg her on, to say all the wrong things and keep her defiant. She'd been so weak in the knees from Junior's wicked and prayerful influence, that Oz welcomed any sign of revolt. If *he* were to give *her* the honest-to-God truth, it would be that he'd been afraid for her for weeks. He'd caught himself obsessively squinting at her pupils, worrying they'd shrunk to pinpoints like a drug addict's; he thought her skin looked splotchy at times, and that her stomach pooched, her hair gone dull, signs of conditions he couldn't bear to know about.

In avoidance of his daughter, Ozzie had spent most recent nights hiding in the studio, the doors locked, the windows blacked-out with trash bags. Since shattering the church window, he'd been immersed in refashioning it into his own rebellion. Word of his crime, his destruction, would quickly spread. Who again would ever trust him with something delicate like the repair of a trumpet played by a glass Gabriel, or the replacement of the broken fold of a saint's robe? But at least this window, if it were his last, would be noticed.

"What if I took you to Nashville myself?" Ozzie said.

"Now, why would you want to do a thing like that?" Charlotte asked, blowing smoke out haughtily.

He didn't want to tell her that Charlotte's mother had spoken, at her sickest, about the three of them taking a trip to Nashville where the country star Rose-Sharon (backed by a trio of chubby women in white pantsuits called the Lilies of the Valley) performed nightly in her own mini-Opry. Rose-Sharon, at the height of her career, had been temporarily silenced by tongue cancer. When she did again sing, with the aid of a prosthesis, it was mostly a high-pitched hum drowned out by the killer pipes of the Lilies of the Valley; nonetheless the ailing flocked from around the world, convinced they'd be healed just from hearing what few peeps they could from the blessed survivor. Jenny mostly joked about such devotion, but Oz could see how enraptured she'd become by the idea of quick-fix miracles. Ever since, he couldn't listen to a Rose-Sharon song on the car radio without having to pull over and blubber.

"We could hunt for Gatling together," Oz told Charlotte.

"You hate Gatling," she said, dismissively, standing, grabbing her purse and snuffing her cig in a slice of birthday cake.

Maybe, when his window was put into place, he'd be declared a heretic, and he and Charlotte would be chased far from town. He was attracted to the idea of a new life somewhere strange. It could conceivably save them, his act of destroying church property.

"Where are you going?" Oz asked.

"Home," she said, leaving the room.

"But I said I would clean up," he called after her.

"So, clean up," she said. The front screen door squeaked open, then slammed shut.

Ozzie walked to the sideboard to splash more bourbon over the fruit in the Widow's glass. As he sipped his drink, he picked up a studio portrait of Tuesday and her family, taken only a few years before, she and Hud and Gatling and Nina sitting stiff-backed in their Sunday garb. Though so much about the portrait seemed forced—from their postures, to their pressed suit jackets and fresh haircuts—Ozzie was jealous. Hud's family looked indestructible. They could all walk out on each other and still never disentangle.

Someone knocked at the front door. "Trick or treat," came a girl's voice, though Halloween was not for another few nights. Ozzie happened to know that Tuesday had a serious sweet tooth for Hot Tamales—for years she'd been buying boxes in bulk from the drive-in's concession stand supplier. As he looked for her stash in the kitchen pantry, he thought of all the elaborate costumes Jenny had sewn for Charlotte's childhood, based on fairy tale characters and historical figures—powdered wigs, endless ruffles, puffy skirts. Charlotte had often wanted to go dressed simply—as a daisy or a bumblebee—but she indulged Jenny, who had always wanted a precocious daughter.

"I don't got all night," came the voice again from the front porch. When Oz went to the door with the box of Hot Tamales, the child gasped. It was Millie, goose-pimpled in a polka-dot bikini and flip-flops, who he hadn't seen since she'd hit the softball through his studio window. Millie dropped her pillowcase of loot and ran into the street, nearly getting sideswiped by a gangly teenaged boy riding a Huffy too small for him. The boy tinkled the bike's bell at her, she called him a faggot, and she wriggled under a row of rose-bushes and vanished. It's not too late to accuse her, he thought, to lie and say that it was her stray ball that had shattered the stained glass. Maybe her sudden appearance on the porch, begging for sugar, was a celestial sign of his last chance at salvation. *She doesn't even know she didn't do it,* whispered the little devil in Oz's left ear.

Oz dismissed the temptation, but not because of any sympathy for Millie. No, he wouldn't pass blame, because then he'd have to give up his plot of rebuilding the window himself—he'd likely have to relinquish all its worthless pieces to the church.

Ozzie sorted through Millie's candy on the porch floor, picking out a few lollipops and some Bazooka, then set the bag inside the front door. He couldn't wait another minute to introduce Charlotte to the wreckage in his studio. Driving home, he pulled up to the sidewalk when he saw her; her long loop of pearls hung down her back, almost reaching the zigzaggy seams of her loose vintage nylons. Charlotte had an artist's spirit, he thought with both pleasure and disappointment.

"I broke the church window," he told her before she'd even closed the pickup door. He handed her a lollipop. "Shattered it. Ruined it."

"How?" she said, gasping, her surprise authentic. *I've got her,* he thought.

"Threw a ball at it."

"On purpose?"

"On purpose," he said. "Kind of on purpose, anyway. But I don't think I was quite in my right mind."

"What are you going to do?"

"Want me to show you?" he asked. Charlotte nodded, and they drove in silence the few blocks to the house. He could tell from the way she chewed on the lollipop, cracking the candy hard on her teeth, that she was nervous. But once they were in the studio, she took on the brisk manner of a woman in charge. She walked to Ozzie's work area, her arms crossed, the authoritative click of her heels echoing.

On a plank of plywood on the floor, Ozzie had begun to jigsaw together his design, meticulously arranging the salvaged shards alongside new pieces of glass. He was working from the bottom up, and had only so far positioned a field of lilies with abstract blooms. Two of the lilies had as their stems the long speckled necks of the giraffes that had originally poked up from the stern of Noah's ark. Another bloomed from the cotton-candy-pink leg that had broken off the biblical stripper Salome. "There had been a choir of angels at the top originally, remember?" he said, kneeling next to the plywood. "But their robes were such a thick white, the morning sunlight would get lost. So I'm using the white glass down here at the bottom." He said nothing of how the flowers suggested Rose-Sharon's loud Lilies of the Valley, or of the other personal references he planned to make. He certainly wouldn't yet tell her about the significance of elevating modest-faced Noah's wife, in the iridescent dress Jenny had so admired, to the very top of the window, graven-image-like, to the red clouds of the revised heaven.

"Where's the cartoon?" Charlotte asked, tapping her foot and glancing around the room before seeing it taped to the wall behind her. Just hearing her use, so unselfconsciously, an inside term like "cartoon"—a stained-glass artist's blueprint, a rendering on paper of a window's design—set Ozzie to picturing Charlotte as his apprentice. As she appraised the drawing, scratching her chin with concentration, Ozzie invented a rosy future for them: Yates & Yates they'd call themselves, or The Oz and Lottie Glass Co.

"Mine is actually a tribute to the original," Oz said, picking up some Polaroids from his workbench. He pointed out to Charlotte the first window's subversive worship—the forked tongue of the snake tickling Eve's naked toes, for example, and the leer of a juggler unicycling through the alleyways of Sodom.

Charlotte only glanced at the photos, and returned her attention to Ozzie's cartoon. He couldn't wait to see her standing in the varied light of the finished window and mesmerized by his Apocrypha—the severed and scattered limbs of biblical figures in turmoil like from the dreams of a fevered priest: Adam's apple on Eve's head; the mummified Lazarus stepping up from the blowhole of Jonah's whale.

"Do you think it's ridiculous?" Oz asked her.

"Yeah," she said, giggling. "Yeah. It's totally ridiculous."

"Well, sure, yeah, it's definitely playful," Oz said. "But I don't know if I, you know, like the idea of it being ridiculous. But yeah, you're probably right, it's maybe too . . . peculiar.

I was afraid of that. It's too ridiculous. What should I change?"

"Oh, no, nothing," Charlotte said. "Nothing at all. It's just crazy. And it's sweet. And you're never going to get away with it."

Then Charlotte, with a spirit he hadn't seen in her in months, maybe years, said, "What if we did go to Nashville?" She picked up a piece of glass that had once been part of a burning bush, and she smoothed her thumb over it. Ozzie intended the flame for the wings of an angel singed by the Apocalypse. "You could open up a shop and sell your own stuff. Not just windows, but lamps. Or sun catchers, and that kind of crap." She glanced back at the cartoon. "Noah's wife at the top. Because Mom liked her dress?"

"How did you know about that?" he said.

"You've told me a million times," she said.

If she were his apprentice, she could convince a congregation of anything, he was certain. She could stand at the altar and articulate that the new window was no act of blasphemy, but rather the exact opposite. *My father has never felt closer to God,* she'd tell them with the gentle fervor of a girl evangelist.

"Sometimes I still have arguments with your mom," Ozzie said. "In my head. Or even out loud sometimes, when I'm alone. I'll think of things we should have fought about more. Like, I still get mad at her for that time she left the back gate open and Darling Clementine ran away. She was always leaving the back gate open. She was so careless a lot of the time." Whenever the gate was open, Clementine, as dumb a dog as any there was, would wander off. And though she was a Great Dane and 120 pounds, she one day just vanished into thin air. Jenny took it the worst, standing in the front of the house in 30-degree cold until midnight, whistling, pacing, like a sailor's wife on the shore gone lunatic. She ended up blaming Oz though, for jinxing the dog, for naming it irresponsibly after the old song that seemed a foretelling: "My darling Clementine, you are lost and gone forever."

"Isn't that stupid?" Oz said. "Old arguments from years ago."

"Ridiculous," Charlotte said, in a voice as tiny as the snap of a twig.

⸙⸙⸙⸙⸙⸙⸙

N I N A bawled nonstop, at the top of her puny lungs, for approximately seventy miles. In the first seat of the school bus, she rested her head on Tuesday's lap and petted the mangy fur collar of her dress in an effort to comfort herself, loosening tiny wild hairs that Tuesday had to occasionally pluck from her own tongue.

Hud tried what he could to quiet her as he drove—he sang a song he composed off-the-cuff, a thing called "Nina's Got No Reasons to Weep," in which he literally sang her praises. Tuesday thought the song was darling but endless.

But, truth be told, for the first fifteen miles or so Tuesday had no interest in calming Nina; had Nina cried herself to sleep too soon, she would have had to pinch the girl to keep her riled up. Hud deserved the guilt. Usually Nina was a too-willing accomplice in Hud's schemes—Tuesday could imagine Nina easily escaping with Hud to Hot Springs and composing her own misleading postcards chronicling her renegade life. It was actually a relief to have Nina so done in by this kidnapping.

Eventually Nina's crying worked to settle Tuesday's anger; as she and Hud suffered together through Nina's noisy nervous breakdown, she found herself needing to exchange exhausted looks in the rearview—they would glance up at each other, smile consolingly, keeping eye contact in the mirror for a moment or two. They didn't share a word, but she knew that he was thinking what she was thinking: of those many long middle-of-the-nights when Nina was newborn and colicky. The squalling baby in his arms, Hud walked in circles in the bedroom, adorable in only his saggy pj bottoms, his hair sticking straight up as he leaned forward to uselessly whisper some coo-cooing in Nina's ear. The infant Nina had been such a brat that Tuesday had gone to the drive-in that first Halloween as Mia Farrow in *Rosemary's Baby*—she'd taken scissors to a blond wig to mimic Mia's Vidal Sassoon hack job and zipped Nina into red terry-cloth jammies on the hood of which she'd sewn little horns.

Tuesday took Nina's mood ring from her finger and put it on her own pinky. At the birthday party they'd all passed the ring around the table, trying it on to watch the clouds in the glass stir into murky telltale colors.

"What does bluish-greenish-yellowish mean?" Tuesday shouted above Nina. "Like a light bruise?" She reached forward and tapped her hand on Hud's arm for him to see. She could have refused to speak to him, or complicated things in any number of ways. She felt she was being generous by not staying in a snit.

"It means you're miserable," Hud shouted back. "Lost. Confused. On the verge in a big way."

Tuesday took her hand back to watch the colors shift again, some pink bubbling up. "I'm not miserable at all," she said, and it was mostly true. She was, in large part, happy, somehow.

"What?" Hud asked, Nina's crying finally lowering to a whimper.

"Nothing," she said. She didn't want him to know that she wasn't miserable. She was surprised by how pleased she was at the thought that she might see Gatling soon. In the days before he left, Gatling had only looked at her with disappointment and pity, seemingly seeing a woman far too inept to keep her son in line. And a crooked glance from one of her children was often all it took to sweep her into insecurity. Even Nina's fits, when she'd accuse Tuesday of cruelty for making her put on a jacket or take a bath, sometimes worked to convince her that she was inept at motherhood. It was foolish, but she couldn't deny it: her children could tell her anything about herself, cast a judgment no matter how skewed, and she'd almost always, at least partly, believe them.

Tuesday was careful to keep still so as not to disturb Nina, who had finally stopped crying, whose lips puffed with soft, congested-sounding snores. She leaned over to rest her forehead against the window as the bus's headlights swept across a salvage yard of junked vehicles. She should have stayed furious with Hud, she knew. If Nina had just gone silently along with the snatch-and-grab, Hud would have ignored Tuesday's banging her fists against the bus. He wouldn't have stopped; he wouldn't have shared his discovery of the South Dakota postmark. She should not mistake any of this, she told herself, for something romantic.

"Do you remember that time," Tuesday said, "when we only had Gatling, and we'd been to South Dakota, and we were driving back along this highway after dark? We saw that guy or that kid or whatever he was, on the shoulder of the highway? He was trying to wave us down, and he had a flashlight."

"Ohhhh yeah," Hud said, "I think so. He was stepping up out of the ditch, I think. But he was holding the flashlight in front of himself, wasn't he? Lighting himself up so we could see him? He was either a short man or a tall boy."

"I don't think he was crawling up out of the ditch," Tuesday said. "He was standing there, standing still, waving one arm really slowly. And I think he was smiling. You know, now that I think about it, *that's* what was so creepy about him. I think that's why we didn't stop." That upsetting smile, sudden and brightly lit, had lingered in the car with them that night, for hours disrupting their sense of safety. "Why do you think he was there?"

"To murder us and steal our damn car," Hud said, too loud.

"Shhh," Tuesday said as Nina shifted on her lap and blinked her eyes open. Tuesday held as still as she could and bit her lip, hoping for Nina to just drift back off. When Nina did close her eyes again, Tuesday said softly, "Or maybe he lived in one those houses out there in the middle of nowhere and needed a ride to the next town. There could have been an emergency. Maybe he wasn't smiling at all and just looked like he was smiling. We drove by so quickly."

"Nah," Hud said. "He had a straight razor in his back pocket that he intended on holding to some poor sucker's throat, I guarantee. Or his junkie girlfriend was crouching in the ditch with a pistol. And we had borrowed your dad's Caddy for the trip, which was pretty new at the time. Leather seats. That fancy climate control that it's got. If we'd have been the ones to be good Samaritans, we'd still be rattling around in that trunk."

"Wouldn't you want someone like us to stop for Gatling if he crawled up out of a ditch? Wouldn't you feel better knowing that respectable people don't just drive by, afraid, when they see some kid needing help?"

"Sure," Hud said. "But I also feel pretty good knowing that I didn't read in the paper the next morning about me and my little family being disemboweled by a hitchhiker. Obviously, if we'd stopped for the kid, and he'd offed us all, Gatling would never have even had a chance to grow up and run away from us. And to crawl up out of a ditch himself someday."

"Ack," Tuesday said, shaking her head at him in the mirror. "The way your brain works." But Tuesday, against her better sense, felt somewhat relieved by Hud's logic and his certainty about the hitchhiker's psychosis and threat. She even felt a little blessed at the thought of having cheated death that night by simply ignoring a gesture for help.

ﻬﻬﻬﻬﻬ

S N O W fell in Hot Springs in the early morning. Tuesday and
Nina sat on the deck of the hotel spa on a teak bench, their
legs wrapped with a frayed electrical blanket that popped and
sizzled as it heated up. They looked like pampered dowagers,
both in terry-cloth robes, dryer-fresh towels twisted around
the tops of their heads. A creek, busy with ducks, ran in front
of the deck, and wisps of steam rose from the warm water.
Tuesday held above herself and Nina an umbrella she had
borrowed from the concierge; she concentrated to listen to the
hiss of the heavy flakes as they touched the water's surface, a
sound like the snuffing of a matchstick.

"Why did you and Daddy get a D-V-I-T-O-R-T?" Nina
asked, annoyed.

Tuesday squinted, putting the letters together in her head.
"Where'd you learn how to almost spell that word?" she asked.

"Daddy and I sing that song sometimes," she said. "You
know," then she sang, off-key, "D-R-O-R-I-T-E."

"No," Tuesday said, then corrected, singing, "D-I-V-O-R-C-E." Nina had wanted them all to strike out together that morning—Hud's plan was to poke around in coffee shops, to question the town's old coots who likely knew everybody. But Tuesday's back and neck ached from the bus ride, so when she saw the list of deluxe services offered in the hotel's spa, it had been too tempting to be a little neglectful. Nina had been mollified some by the lemon wedge the spa specialist had given her to suck on (Nina loved things sour enough to make her nose run), but she was still fidgety with disgust.

For all of Tuesday's frustrations with Gatling, she had faith that his return to their lives would restore the old warped order. From the time that Nina was an infant, she and Hud had sided together in family disputes. Hud would get angry with Gatling for some dumb bit of rebellion, and as punishment, he'd lavish all his attention on his little girl. Tuesday sometimes actually felt nostalgic for those days when Hud barely spoke to Gatling, and she and her son would steal moments alone to lament all the dysfunction of their tiny house as they snuck cigarettes in the mudroom or rocked slowly on the backyard swing set. They'd sit there, the chains creaking, staring at the house, at the reflections of the trees in the windows, and inventorying all Hud's failings. All the while they'd be secretly hoping for him to step outside and smile and wave, or bring them some cold bottles of root beer, signaling the end of his fit of bad temper. Hud was not at all cruel, only childish, and stubbornly distant at his worst. And when he was at his worst, everyone around him fell hostage to his mood.

A spa lady in pink scrubs appeared with a mortar and pestle. "So what brings you to Hot Springs?" she asked. The woman began to putty the crushed fruit onto Tuesday's cheeks with a tongue depressor.

"I'm looking for my son," Tuesday told her. She said it like a woman might say it in an English mystery, giving it a tenor of hope and exhaustion and propriety. "His name is Gatling Smith."

Tuesday had already left a message with her school's secretary explaining that she had to attend to a family emergency. As she looked up at the former veteran's hospital on the hillside that towered, abandoned, over the village like a fairy-tale castle, she considered quitting her job. She could become an art therapist in a spa town, she thought. In her years as a grade school art teacher, she'd interpreted hundreds of telling works in crayon and pencil, feeling privy to the children's most deep-seated psychoses. She'd seen stick figures exact bloody violence on father types in neckties, and pretty, chimney-topped houses painstakingly drawn brick by brick only to then be scribbled over with a swirling tornado. Boys had articulated the intricacies of complicated guns, every trigger and switch, while girls had rendered themselves entirely without faces in family portraits.

"Do you have a picture of your son?" the woman asked, obscuring Tuesday's vision by placing a few thin slices of cucumber over her eyes.

Before leaving to comb Hot Springs, Hud had given Tuesday one of the two outdated wallet-sizes of Gatling that he always carried around with him. Both pictures were creased and water-speckled. Hud took Gatling age seven, front teeth missing, stubborn cowlick, suede vest. Tuesday took Gatling age twelve with a bowl-like haircut he'd probably never forgive her for.

"I've got it," Nina said. She had kept it at hand all morning.

"But imagine him almost eighteen now," Tuesday said, lifting a cucumber slice to watch for the woman's reaction.

"They have computer programs that can, you know, do a time-lapse thingie," she said, handing it back. "You know. Make them look like they might look. Did his dad run off with him?"

"No," Tuesday said, though she was tempted to say *yes* so she wouldn't have to admit that she had simply let Gatling slip away. "Gatling's tall. Pretty blue eyes. And these long, dark lashes I'd kill for. And he has this kind of pompadour, I guess you'd call it?" She smoothed her fingers over the top of her head, as if signing the international symbol for "pompadour." "I've always hated that haircut," Tuesday added. She laughed. "He'd look so much better with it just normal. Oh, and he has a tattoo on his arm. Dice." She didn't tell the woman about the scars across his chest; she didn't want her to judge.

"A friend of my sister's," the woman said, nodding, and Tuesday's pulse sped up.

"Gatling's a friend of your sister's?" she asked.

"Oh, no, no, sorry, dear," she said. "A friend of my sister's got her kid snatched." She took a file to the fingernails of Tuesday's broken hand. "A little boy named . . ." She *hmmmed*, twisting her lips around in semi-deep thought. "Freddie?

Frankie? Anyway, it's been, like, four years. The boy's dad took him on a hunting trip and didn't bring him back, and now who the hell knows? About a year later, there was a message on my sister's friend's answering machine that might have been from the kid, but all it was was a tiny little voice saying a single word—what sounded like 'Mommy?' We all sat there and listened and listened, and one of us would think we heard it clearly, so we'd play it back, then play it again, then we'd start to think it wasn't even a voice at all, but like the squeak of a bedspring. Or a bird tweeting. It was like when a word's at the tip of your tongue. It was like at the tip of your ear, you know? The tip of your hearing. But before she could even bring the answering machine to the police, she lost the message. It was just on one of those microchips, and it got recorded over when her boyfriend called to yell at her for not coming over to walk his dog. Can you believe it? Trash."

Her eyes shut behind the cuke slices, Tuesday instinctively reached a pinky out, just to feel Nina beside her. "Did your sister's friend ever suspect that her ex would run off with Freddie? Frankie?" Tuesday asked.

"I don't think so," she said. "He had a cushy job. He'd just bought new boobs for his fiancée. Things were looking up for him."

All morning Tuesday's patience with Hud had wavered—when he'd brought her a change of clothes from a hardware store, she'd at first been flattered that the Levis didn't fit, implying that he thought she was much thinner in the hips than she actually was. But then she'd gotten miffed, wishing he knew her better, that he'd ever bothered to notice that she wasn't the same insanely petite thing he'd married. Then, as they'd headed around the corner to a café with lace drapes to have cinnamon bear claws, she'd put her arm in his in front of a place called Mad Hattie's Haberdashery. In the window, on a mannequin, was a dress of crushed blue velvet.

"I might go as Isabella Rossellini this year," Tuesday speculated. "You could go as Dennis Hopper. You could wear an oxygen mask; that might be cute." She knew she shouldn't encourage any hope for a return to old times, but something about seeing her breath in the cold morning air made her nostalgic. For years the drive-in had played its last movie of the season on Halloween, people showing up in costume to sit through a wretched horror flick from Red's collection. Hud had once chosen to go in t-shirt and cuffed jeans as Paul Le Mat, an actor he regarded as underrated, in *American Graffiti,* with Tuesday as his Mackenzie Phillips. After sending the kids to the drive-in's office to play Monopoly with the Widow, Hud and Tuesday, though having barely touched their thermos full of grape juice and vodka, kissed and heavy-petted in the backseat.

Dressing up as movie couples had become one of their own traditions, and Hud had always longed for tradition, Tuesday knew. He'd admired how Tuesday's family was so close-knit and shut off, with their own words for things and their own odd habits on holidays. Standing in front of Mad Hattie's Haberdashery, wrapping her arms around Hud for warmth, she'd realized how much she'd probably upset him by not inviting him to Rose's stupid party. And in the chill and the slow snowfall, in this town with its healthful waters, she felt like forgiving him, and overlooking for the moment his capacity for making a hash of everything. If he ended up agreeing to go as Dennis Hopper to her Isabella Rossellini, she thought she might even be able to entertain the idea of inching toward reconciliation.

DESPITE flashing Gatling's old school picture around and offering explicit description, down to the chicken-pock mark to the left of his left eye and the oval burn scar on his ankle from once touching against the hot muffler of a refurbed moped when he was eleven, Hud gathered nothing from the coffee-shop gossips. But he was buoyed by the attention the strangers gave him, and their sympathetic gestures of buying him cup after cup of bitterly strong joe as he sat right down at their tables to tell them the story of losing his family.

The only person to offer a clue of where to begin to look was a woman who sat on the porch of a bed and breakfast, with an easel and paints, wearing a yellowed white-fur coat. Though the woman cast her gaze down the street and up a cliff, she painted an old boat abandoned to a lake.

"Try Mad Hattie's Haberdashery," the woman said upon hearing about the postcards Gatling had been sending. "She has a collection of postcards from all over. I bought one once—a nifty holograph of a pagoda. When you moved it a little, Japanese girls stood and bowed."

When Mad Hattie's finally opened at noon, Hud, who'd been waiting on a bench, stepped in feeling ice-cold, his head filled with the noise of his teeth clacking. "I want to buy that dress in the window," he told the only person inside. The woman stood adjusting the coat-hanger rabbit ears of a black-and-white TV in an effort to bring in a soap opera—the noise in the room moved back and forth between syrupy violin strings and static.

"I'll tell you right now it's not going to fit," the woman deadpanned. Though she wore a baseball jersey with Evel Knievel on it, and pajama bottoms patterned with cacti and coiled rattlesnakes, Hud mistook her for a serious person.

"It's not for me," he said.

The woman sighed and moved toward the window display. "I know," she said, not pleasantly. "I'm a little bit of a comedian." The zipper on the blue velvet dress stuck, so she ended up dismantling the mannequin, unscrewing the hands from the wrists, the waist from the hips. The woman cussed up a storm as she struggled with the parts of the dummy.

Hud refused to let the woman's sourness affect his temper. There'd been no sign yet of Gatling in Hot Springs, but in the hours since sunup Hud had been nearly delirious with contentment. When Tuesday slipped her arm in his in front of the window of Mad Hattie's, when she'd proposed going out on Halloween as another sick movie couple, it had been all he could do to keep an ounce of cool. In his enthusiasm, he'd nearly ruined the moment by rattling off other costume suggestions—Hud had always preferred to go as someone who looked good, like James Dean in *Giant,* with Tuesday as Liz Taylor, in the scene where Dean serves her tea in his shack.

"You want the velvet shoes too?" the woman asked.

"Why not?" Hud said. "So are you Hattie, or what?"

"People call me Trish," she said. She took the dress and shoes to a roll-top desk, where she stapled a rip in a seam, then began to color in scuff marks on the shoes with a mascara brush. "Hattie was just the name already on the window when I bought the place."

Hud saw the spinning rack of postcards across the room; he went to thumb through them, picking up one featuring a cartoon 'gator in a tux wishing greetings from the Florida Everglades, and a naughty one with a naked lady in a beret sitting at a sidewalk bistro in Paris. Just as he was about to ask Trish if a boy named Gatling frequented Mad Hattie's, he saw the guitar—midnight blue with Nina's name in yellow in quotation marks painted along a curve.

"Oh my God," Hud said, more relieved than shocked, picking the guitar up from where it sat perched in the bowl of a dry stone birdbath. The beaded strap held the scent of Gatling's skin, a mix of Brut cologne and sweat. Hud put the strap around his shoulder and strummed a few chords, then tightened the strings to tune. "How the hell'd you get this?" he asked.

"Oh," Trish said, "Charlotte." In a split second Hud conjured up a whole conspiracy, Charlotte tiptoeing up to Hot

Springs for weekends on the sly, inventing theories of Nashville to throw everyone off. "That's what we call him, anyway," she said, "because that's what it says on the poor thing's chest. He works as an afternoon lifeguard over at the indoor Plunge. He doesn't talk to anyone much, so I don't think anyone even knows his real name."

Hud hugged his son's guitar to his chest and ran his cheek against the neck of it. No wonder no one had responded to Hud's description of the boy—he'd left off the scars, he realized. He'd totally forgotten. He'd been simply describing a big-eyed, misguided youth likely making a living as a street musician. A nomadic troubadour.

"This might interest you too," Trish said, opening a drawer in a curio cabinet. "I keep these out of sight. I'm not sure what to charge for them." She held up a plastic baggy containing a pair of white panties. "Used," she said. "And even signed by the bad Daughter of God, believe it or not." She opened the baggy and took from it a Polaroid that she held up for Hud to see. In it, the Daughter of God named Sunny, with a dirty grin, lifted her choir robe to show the very same white panties now preserved at Mad Hattie's Haberdashery. "Can't ask for more authentication than that," she said. She touched her fingertip to the photo, to Sunny's privates.

"Just add this guitar to the dress and shoes, please," he said with a strum.

"What's your interest in it, anyway?" she asked.

"The guy you call Charlotte is my son," he said. He played a few chords of "A Boy Named Sue."

After putting the dress and shoes in a grocery sack, Trish lit up a cigarette and crossed her legs. She seemed to study Hud's face a moment. He thought she might be seeking a resemblance. "I have a fifteen-year-old daughter who won't even get her curls wet at the Plunge," she said, "though your boy doesn't look in her direction. Thank God. My Sylvie would escape with him in a second if he said a word. It's bad enough that he's kind of pretty, but he's got that precious-innocent look on his face. And with that girl's name gouged into his chest? Forget it. He could be lethal to a dumb kid like mine."

"Well, whatever," Hud said, with pride in his son's aura of mystery and trouble. "I'll be taking him away. He'll be going home with me."

"Don't sneak up on him, for God's sake," she said. "You don't want to spook him, so don't go waltzing to the Plunge expecting a big 'Good to see ya.' Leave him a note. Tell him where you are. Let him come to you."

Hud was tempted to take her advice—Trish had silver hairs and dark circles beneath her eyes, and had begun to speak in the grave voice of a woman who'd seen more than a few things through to their worst possible conclusions.

GATLING slouched in a low lifeguard's chair at the edge of the indoor pool, looking not at all like the devil-may-care, soulful-eyed boy Hud had been describing around town. When Hud saw that he'd buzzed his thick hair to the skin of his skull and that he'd grown thinner in the seven or so months since running off, he nearly turned and snuck out.

"If I was a drowning man," Hud called out, "I'd have to call for a priest. Look at yourself." Gatling appeared unfit to rescue even himself if forced to leap into the deep end—he was lucky if he weighed a good 130 pounds soaking wet. Hud had intended for his greeting to sound kind of slap-on-the-back, all buddy-buddy, unceremonious. But his voice trembled and echoed off the walls.

Gatling looked up, smiling, not a flicker of shock on his face. "Hey, Pops," he said with a wink. He too seemed to want to come across as the king of smooth, but then he bit his lip and looked back down toward the water, his shoulders beginning to shake. Hud stopped at the sound of Gatling's sniffling, still several steps from the lifeguard's chair. He clenched his teeth and rubbed his tongue against the roof of his mouth, then remembered you did that to keep from sneezing, not to keep from crying.

"I didn't mean it, Gup," he said, resurrecting an old nickname, short for "Guppy," he hadn't used in years. The few times Hud had brought his family to Hot Springs for vacation, they'd spent most of their days in the 80-degree waters of the Plunge, Gatling the most content to abolish all plans of sightseeing the Badlands and Mount Rushmore and even the Reptile Gardens, where Nina had hoped to rub elbows with defanged vipers. More than once, in the thick air of the indoor pool, Gatling had upset them all with his talent for dead-man-floating so convincingly.

"Nah, come on, kid, you look svelte," Hud said, sniffling now himself. "The girls go for scrawny these days, right?" He didn't want Gatling to feel too bad, but he certainly didn't want him to feel too good. After all, he hoped to convince Gatling to move into his bachelor pad with him, where he could fatten him up with steaks and beer as dark as molasses.

Gatling tipped himself forward and dropped into the water with a splash that rocked a toddler in her turtle-shaped inner tube, sending her slightly, merrily floating away from her mother, who leaned against a wall of the pool immersed in a paperback. Hud walked to the edge and squatted to watch Gatling gently kick his legs to keep beneath the surface. Hud remembered the afternoon at the Plunge when Tuesday lost a heart-shaped locket he'd just bought for her from a souvenir shop that sold Black Hills gold. Inside the tiny thing, she'd put Nina's lips, cut from a photo she'd had in her purse, and Gatling's right eye. Hud and Gatling had taken deep breaths and plumbed the shallow depths, running their hands along stones and turning them over, hoping to feel the locket's gold chain catch in their fingers like thin strings of seaweed.

Hud now put his hand in the water. Gatling reached up and touched Hud's fingertips with his own. After a moment, Hud took hold of Gatling's hand and tugged. Gatling floated, face first, to the surface, his eyes shut. He then crossed his arms on the edge of the pool and rested his chin on one elbow. Hud ran the flat of his hand over Gatling's buzz cut, then gave his boy's head a light rub with his knuckles. He wanted to wrap him in a towel and cradle him in his arms until he stopped shivering.

"How'd you know where I was?" Gatling asked. Hud touched Gatling's earlobe, then the freckled skin of his shoulder, then the back of his neck.

"The postmarks on your notes from your so-called travels," Hud said. "Then some woman named Trish at that Mad Hattie's sold me this." He reached behind himself to thump the guitar he carried there. "I got it back for you."

"Ack," Gatling said. He lowered his head, hiding his eyes in his arms. "Do me a big favor and smash the hell out of it. Rip it apart string by string. Prolong its agony."

"That's not what you want." Hud hoped he'd never been the type of father to discourage his son's ambitions, though he knew he'd never been one to fuss, like a father probably ought to fuss, over the dippy soft-country songs Gatling wrote. Gatling's writing, in Hud's opinion, tended toward greeting-card sentiment—too many sunsets, too much moonlight. But sometimes something more would rise above the clutter of love stuff. His best song, one he wrote for Charlotte called "A Girl in a Tire Swing Eating a Pear," seemed to capture something exact about the girl's sadness. Gatling had only ever sung it once for Hud.

"I barely know how to even play a guitar right," Gatling said. "Take it back to Mad Hattie's. Some knucklehead can pick it up and start his own crappy band."

"See, that just kills your old dad. To hear that tone in your voice. What didn't I do for you, Gup? Why did you come here instead of coming home?"

"I'm a failure," Gatling said.

"You're not a failure," Hud said. "Not one bit of a failure. I admire you. I want to be you. Y'know? When I grow up, I guess." He laughed, but Gatling said nothing for a moment. He just rubbed his thumb against the toe of Hud's boot.

"The Daughters of God gave me my walking papers up in Fargo," Gatling said. "We'd stopped to do a concert for a woman who got shot in the head twice and lived. She shows off her bullet holes and people freak. Stella, that's the manager, she didn't like it that I'd been messing around with Sunny, so she gave me the heave-ho. But I shouldn't complain, I suppose. They were good to me, while things were fine."

Hud ran his hand down to touch the scars on Gatling's chest. He closed his eyes, hoping that he wouldn't be able to feel the letters if he wasn't looking right at them.

"Get out of the pool," Hud said, his voice shivery again. Then he felt a shot of almost otherworldly strength and energy, maybe that superhuman adrenaline rush you sometimes read about, when men find themselves capable of pushing cars off the tops of their broken wives, or jumping into frozen-over river rapids to rescue a little girl. Hud felt compelled to knock Gatling unconscious and drag him away by the nape of the neck if he had to. "Your mom and Nina are back at the hotel. They'll croak when they see you walk in. Come on. Out."

Gatling giggled, tickled, as Hud put his hands beneath his arms in an effort to pull him up. He slapped Hud's hands away. "Stop, Pops. Cool it." He pushed himself off the wall of the pool and floated on his back a few feet away, serene ripples lifting and lowering his body. "I've got to finish my shift. They've been good to me here. I don't want to leave them in the lurch. I'll meet you guys at your hotel in a couple of hours."

Hud was frightened to let Gatling out of his sight for even a second now that he'd found him, but then Gatling swam back to the edge, muscles moving beneath the skin of his shoulders. "I'm not going to ditch you, Pops," Gatling said, reaching up to offer a painfully hard handshake that belied his new frailty. "Why would I do that, old man? I'm no worthless kid at heart."

2 3 .

TUESDAY cranked up the heat of the hotel room to a fever-
ish peak, and she allowed everyone wine, even Nina, who
drank a few sips from Gatling's glass. They'd all dressed up to
go out, but when Gatling arrived so pencil-thin, strangled by
a gaudy necktie with a crooked knot, Tuesday cried just
enough to make a mess of her little bit of makeup. The weeping was unexpected, but she welcomed it. It felt like maternal
instinct.

They'd decided to cancel their reservations and splurge on
room service; the floor was now littered with empty bottles,
and plates with picked-clean T-bones.

"My glass is filthy," Gatling said, squinting, in his tipsiness, at the gray ghost of a lipstick print. He held the glass up
to the glow of the lamp—Tuesday had dimmed way down the
room's light.

"Nah, it's that stay-on lipstick the girls wear now," Hud
said. "It's a serious problem for Augustine at the lounge. You

could scrub at that glass for hours and get nowhere." Hud lay alone on the other bed in a laughably yellow suit he'd picked up at Mad Hattie's on his way back to the hotel, the only suit in the shop that had fit decent.

"I'm wearing Mom's lipstick," Nina said, puckering up.

"Just for tonight," Tuesday said.

"Gimme a smudge," Gatling said, tapping a finger against his cheek. Nina hadn't left his side since he arrived, her head now next to his on a pillow. She kissed him lightly, then harder, neither kiss leaving much of a mark. Then everyone devoted their attention to getting Nina's lip print on Gatling's cheek, with Tuesday painting Nina's lips and Hud advising on smooching technique. Finally Nina had covered both Gatling's cheeks with expert lipstick splotches.

"Here's a place for you, Mom," Nina said, pointing at a naked spot on Gatling's forehead.

But Tuesday just put the lid on the tube and dropped it into the nightstand drawer. "Lipstick ain't cheap, honey," she said, though she'd only paid 79 cents for it at the drugstore next to the hotel, and had had to make do with an orangey tint of coral, the only shade left.

She noticed Hud drifting off to sleep, the glass of wine in his hand beginning to teeter. Tuesday carefully lifted the glass from his fingers, then returned to sitting on the edge of the other bed, to drink the rest of his wine.

Gatling, Nina's head now resting on his stomach, played with the loose thread of a seam up the side of Tuesday's blue velvet dress, and she held still, pretending not to notice. She was afraid if she noticed, he might stop.

"Please tell me I'm not the reason you're staying away from home," Tuesday told Gatling.

Gatling shook his head and smiled sympathetically, running his finger over Nina's sweat-soaked bangs. "Nobody's the reason," he said. Nina's eyes blinked rapidly, then she was asleep too.

"I know I can be vindictive sometimes, maybe, but that's not anything I like about myself," Tuesday continued. "That's not even me. It's just my mother coming through in me. That's the way *she* is. Unforgiving. Punishing." She refilled Gatling's glass, though his eyes were wet and heavy-lidded. This felt like the thump of maternal instinct too, this need to drug her family with wine and warmth, to keep them all asleep in this cramped room in winter.

"Are you and Dad back together?" Gatling asked.

"No," Tuesday said. "He has the room across the hall." Hud had rolled over, his back to them, fetaled up and breathing slow. For years Tuesday had worried about herself in old age, were Hud to go first, and what it would be like to wake all alone every day, in your terrible last years when you needed your husband the most. But now they were divorced, and all those worries were replaced with others. She missed that old anxiety, with an ache in her stomach.

"What really happened to your hand?" Gatling asked. Though Tuesday had all along been entirely opposed to lying about how her hand broke, when Gatling had first asked, only moments after seeing her again, she'd found herself stuttering, claiming to have tripped into a wall. Even Nina kept silent, Nina, who lived for ratting out people who fibbed.

"I don't want to get into it," she said. "It's complicated. You know, you can't leave, then just show up out of nowhere, expecting answers."

"I didn't show up out of nowhere," he said. "You came to me. Here I was, minding my own business."

"Come home with us, baby," she said. She took a tissue and licked it, then began to dab at Gatling's cheeks to wash away Nina's sloppy kisses. Gatling laughed and gently pushed her hand away. "Charlotte misses you too. I know she does."

"That sucks for Charlotte," Gatling said. "Because I don't miss her. I've got other girls to miss now."

Tuesday was relieved to hear the touch of spite in his voice. "It's for the best, maybe," she said. "It's probably good when you can leave young love behind you. It doesn't age well."

Gatling rolled his eyes, clucked his tongue. He spoke softly, almost whispering. "You love to say things that I don't want to hear, don't you?"

"What did I say that you don't want to hear?" she said, whispering now too.

"I don't know," he said. He gently lifted Nina away from him so that he could sit upright next to Tuesday. "When I was a kid. I mean, the things you thought were OK to say to me . . ." He shook his head, disapproving.

"I know there was stuff I did wrong," she said, "but you have to know that my heart was in the right place."

"Well, sometimes it seems to me that maybe your heart was, really, just nowhere even near where it needed to be. Do you remember this one time, I was, like, five, or six, and I don't think I was even doing anything, I mean, I don't think I was being a brat, or anything, I was just sitting there eating a cookie, and you said to me, out of nowhere, I can hear it, you said, 'Honey, I almost gave you up for adoption when you were born. I don't want there to be any secrets. So I'm telling you right now, I had every intention of giving you up for adoption. And as much as I love you, and I love you to death, that probably would've been the best thing for all of us. We probably both would've had a better life.' It was just like that. I mean, goddamn, Mom. I was *five*."

Tuesday had no recollection of it. She could barely picture Gatling at five years old. It seemed he'd always been a surly teen. But even if she had said exactly that, hadn't she said she loved him to death? She looked over at Hud, who either slept soundly or feigned sleep to avoid taking a stand. She was tempted to wake him and demand that he defend her. He owed her big for the night before; when she had seen him lift Nina from the dining room chair during Rose's party, her heart had sped up with fear and filled with certainty that he and Nina would never return.

"Maybe I didn't always say the right things," Tuesday said, "but cut me some slack, why don't you? I was barely older than you are now."

"Yeah, well, if I had a kid of my own now, I'd never let him know how miserable I am."

"You'll be a great father someday," she said, not wanting to bicker. She put her hand on his chest, pleased to feel the lines of scars beneath his shirt. The name cut into his skin, damage so self-inflicted, was a living sign that Tuesday and Hud weren't responsible for all the boy's injury. He was far too sensitive.

"Come home with us," Tuesday said again. "We'll talk it all out."

Gatling smiled wide and shook his head. "What is home, anyway? Where would I stay? With you? Dad? You'd probably fight about it." Gatling gave his mother a hug and a kiss on the cheek. "Besides, I have a girl here in town, and I want it to work out. Speaking of being a father. She's got a two-year-old who's kind of getting attached to me."

"How long have you even . . ."

"We've been hanging out for about a month. The kid's a doll-baby. Talks all the time but doesn't know a word. Jabbers his own little language."

"A month."

He took a folded-up snapshot from his wallet, a picture of him with the boy on his knee, sitting on the back of a rusty white Pinto with vanity plates that said *SPOIL ME*. "That's Jasmine's shadow stretching across the ground there," Gatling said. "She was taking the picture. That's her car. I'd say you could meet her, but she's even more of a chatterbox than her kid. We'd never get a word in edgewise." Now that Gatling was talking about the chatty Jasmine and her son, he no longer seemed sleepy or drunk, or even morose or angry. He hopped over onto the other bed to shake his father awake, then to kiss his dad's neck and wrap his arms around him.

"Sorry to bore you right to sleep, Pops," Gatling said.

"No," Hud said. "No. It's just been a long couple of days. Why'd you let me drift off?"

"It's fine," Gatling said, standing and plucking the photo from Tuesday's hand, and sticking it back in his pocket. "Me and the mother of your children have just been doing a little catching up." He winked at Tuesday as he stepped backward toward the door, nervously clapping his hands together, looking like a man flat broke trying to weasel away from a poker game gone awry.

"Should we meet for breakfast?" Hud asked. "You still have a chocolate doughnut and Pepsi every morning?"

"Nah," he said. "Jasmine's a health nut. Just hot cereal and banana mush for me these days. Besides, we're actually going out of town tomorrow. True story, honest to God. Leaving at the crack of dawn. Taking her kid down to see her mom and twin sister in Boulder, Colorado." He looked at his watch, but he didn't seem to see the time at all. "Matter of fact, Jazzy and the kid are probably watching the clock right now, waiting for me. Tell Nina there that I kissed her while she slept. You know me, never had the stomach for good-byes."

"Now wait a minute, Gup," Hud said as both he and Tuesday stood.

Gatling opened the door. Smiling, he reached out to slap Hud's shoulder. "Pops, you know where to find me now. You'll come up and you'll check on me from time to time. I'm not going anywhere, I swear to God. I'm staying put. Not moving an inch. I promise." With that, he was gone with a skip into the hall.

Hud sat on the end of the bed, and after a quiet minute or two picked up Gatling's guitar from the floor. "Should I chase after him and give him this?" he asked. "Or go get him and drag him back? Kicking. Screaming." He then began to hum and mumble the words *kicking* and *screaming,* stretching them out, and he played a few pleasing notes. "Who's Jasmine? Who's her kid?"

"New people," Tuesday said. She rumpled Hud's hair as she passed. At the window, she watched the snow fall like rain in the light of a streetlamp. She worried about Gatling out in such weather. Then she dreaded another winter in her little drafty house with its ice-cold walls. When she had first married Hud, she'd fretted that neither of them was resourceful enough to keep their old house from falling down around them all. Even as a little girl she'd wondered if she would have been as clever as Gretel, capable of tricking the witch into her own stove.

ⵊⵊⵊⵊⵊ

H U D dropped off a disposable camera for one-hour developing late the next morning, Nina having been a frenzied shut-
terbug the night before, snapping shots of Gatling even as he
gnawed on his steak and spilled wine on his pants.

During the wait Hud and Tuesday and Nina toured a fos-
sil excavation site; still tired and preoccupied, they moved
sluggishly across scaffolding along the edge of a pit where
mammoths had perished eons before. The beasts had stepped
out of the cold winds of an ice age into a pool of hot spring
water for a luxurious soak, a guide explained, only to find
themselves unable to scale back up the muddy walls. Now
this mass grave was bone dry and covered and climate con-
trolled, and spotlit for anthropologists.

Nina walked between Hud and Tuesday, holding both
their hands, as they moved along the path, glancing down at
the men and women below dusting off tusks and pelvic gir-
dles lodged in silt. "Is Gatling coming home with us?" Nina

asked. She wore a black fright wig with streaks of white that Hud had bought for her from a bin of quick-discount Halloween costumes at the drugstore.

"Nope," Tuesday said. "You know," she said to Hud, "he told me I told him too much when he was a kid. Revealed too much. And maybe I did. Before Nina came along, we were alone together a lot. I probably did confide in him."

Hud, however, thought Tuesday held her tongue too often for her own good. If she'd spoken up more during their marriage, maybe he would have better understood her unhappiness. Instead she would use up her fight, hushed, on the kitchen phone with her sister, Rose, guzzling coffee or cotton-balling old polish from her nails.

"Shhh, you're rude," Nina said, dropping their hands and stepping forward to be nearer the guide. And it was rude, Hud supposed, to be talking; there were only two other people in the group, the place practically a ghost town in the off season.

"I wonder if I'll get fired for taking that rattletrap of a bus," Hud whispered close to Tuesday's ear. He took her hand. Her fingers were loose in his at first, but then he felt them tighten, and he felt her lean against him. "I wonder how the kids got to school this morning," he said. "By spring I want to be in a better position. I want Nina to be able to rely on me for things. I'm going to look into this freelance gig one of the other bus drivers was telling me about. He's making forty bucks a phone call to tell farmers that their health insurance is tripling."

As the guide described how hunters would follow the migration of their prey, erecting huts built from the rib cages and hides of giant bears and woolly mammoths, Nina scrambled ahead, then tried to pull herself up to see better over the railing. "Pssst," Hud hissed in her direction, snapping his fingers at her, gesturing for her to get down. He could just imagine her tumbling over and into the pit. Cracking her head open on a skull bone. "I wouldn't have run off with Nina alone the other night," Hud told Tuesday. "I would've just driven around the block until I cooled off."

"I know," Tuesday said.

"I would never take Nina away from you," he said.

"I know," she said. She squeezed his hand a few times before letting go. He was fairly certain she believed him.

Before leaving Hot Springs that afternoon, Hud paid what he considered a rather cruelly exorbitant price for the rest of Gatling's belongings at Mad Hattie's. They then stopped at the Plunge, to call Gatling's bluff, but the boy had indeed taken some days off, they were told, and Nina left him a plea to come home, in her sloppy handwriting, all her "i's" dotted with hearts.

The weather worsened, and they drove a few long hours in snow and sleet, the roads frightening and slick. All the nervous breath in the bus fogged the window, requiring that Hud often lean forward to wipe at the window with the end of his sleeve. "Ease up on the breathing, girls," he said, to make light, but Tuesday and Nina were too anxious to laugh. When the stretches of snow on the land gave way to the return of the yellows and wines and reds of autumn, and the start of the sunset riddled the clouds with shots of light, the mood in the bus lifted. It lifted so much that Tuesday ended up in the aisle teaching Nina a dusty old line dance from the days when she and Hud would drive up the highway to the now-defunct Swift Kick Saloon where, in the parking lot, Mexican strippers peddled hot car stereos and VCRs.

But, to their surprise, as they neared home, they drove back into snow and ice. Though it wasn't unusual for South Dakota to see winter before the end of fall, it had snowed in October in their Nebraska town only a few times that Hud could remember. Tuesday and Nina sat behind Hud, clicking their tongues with shock at the sight of all the ravaged trees. The branches had not yet dropped all their leaves and couldn't bear the additional weight of the icicles and heavy snow.

The drive-in's marquee promoted its annual Halloween costume party and a double bill of schlock, *She-Freak* and *Shriek of the Mutilated,* but the place sat dark and unplowed, its gate padlocked. Some of the residential streets of the town were closed, blocked off by broken branches or snapped power lines or whole trees that had split down their middles. It was early evening, after dark, but there were no trick-or-treaters around, only Millie steering her bike in the street around branches and patches of ice and snow; she wore a toy tiara and a pink gown that looked made of paper. One of the few porch lights lit was Nanette Schrock's. Hanging in front of the light was a puppetlike witch decoration. With her loosely hinged joints, the witch did an impromptu soft-shoe in the night wind, casting quivering shadows across the drifts on Nanette's lawn.

Hud pulled up in front of the home of Ozzie and Charlotte, the photos from the night before in his back pocket. He wanted to offer Charlotte proof, and to tempt her toward Hot Springs with a sight of Gatling's skin-and-boniness, to appeal to her sense of drama. Though Gatling had another girl now, there was simply no denying an old love whose name was splayed, like a bloody crime, across your flesh.

A note was taped over the doorbell. "Gone to Nashville," it said, and it was signed by both Oz and Charlotte. Hud was skeptical, though all the lights of the house were out and the pickup gone from the drive. Hud selected a photo in which Gatling looked the perfect mix of lost lamb and rebel soul, and he slipped it beneath the door.

"The mayor canceled Halloween earlier today," Tuesday explained as Hud got back on the bus. Tuesday sat in the driver's seat, having tuned the AM radio to a local station. "A lot of people are still without electricity."

Nina moped with the fright wig in her lap. "Well, I'm not so sure the mayor has the authority to cancel Halloween," Hud said. "What's to cancel? You knock on people's doors and they either give you candy or they don't. I say we act in defiance of the mayor! It's revolution!" He put Nina's wig back on her head.

Their revolution consisted only of going back to the house for their own private Halloween party. Tuesday put her blue velvet dress and shoes back on. Nina decided to be one of the teenaged tramps that loitered at the drive-in in the summer, so she put on a tube top and some cutoffs and sparkled her cheeks with spray-on glitter. Hud just put on one of his dad's old suits, musty from having been abandoned in the basement. When they discovered a mysterious pillowcase containing a scant amount of sweets, just sitting atop the trunk by the front door, they couldn't have been more tickled if the bag had been filled with something useful. Nina divvied up the candy, and Hud told a ghost story about a disembodied eyeball, but he found himself unable to remember the ending of it.

After a dinner of microwave popcorn and Hot Tamales, Hud gentlemanly excused himself, pinching Nina's shimmering cheek, then kissing it. Tuesday walked him to the front door.

"Did I tell you I got blackjacked coming out of the lounge the other night?" Hud asked. He turned the back of his neck to Tuesday, and she pushed down on his collar. She pressed his bruise, and he cringed from the jolt of pain.

"Sorry," she said, snapping her hand back with a little laugh. "A lot of bad luck in that parking lot," she said, waving her cast. Tuesday crossed her arms and shivered from the cold let in by the open door. "Thanks for getting us home safely tonight. Those roads were tricky. I could tell you were really white-knuckling it."

"I was nervous," he said. He wanted to kiss her quick, but instead reached up to push some fine strands of hair from her cheek.

"Come back in the morning early and shovel the walk," Tuesday said. "I'll fix you breakfast after."

"It'll have to be early early," Hud said. "I've got to get all those kids to school."

"Early early's good," she said, and there was that pause when there could've been a kiss, but Hud thought it more gallant to simply wink.

It was funny to Hud, as he drove back to his apartment, that he could be so looking forward to a morning so dismal, to breaking his back scooping snow in the cold, especially when he recalled all the years of battle over such things—the squabbling over leaky faucets and cracks in windows, over who dressed what kid last, who drove who where, all the empty whats and whens that had slowly turned him and Tuesday against each other.

Hud drove past the church with a panel of wood covering its missing window—across the wood someone had spray-painted *JESUS IS WITH YOU* in black, and the sight of it was startling in a way the stained glass never had been.

Then Hud's headlights swept across a kid dressed in the red long johns of some superhero, his sleeves stuffed to simulate bulging muscles. The kid tossed toilet paper into a severed tree limb on the ground, stringing the paper among icicles, then disappeared around a corner. As Hud drove slowly toward the town square, he caught glimpses of other covert trick-or-treaters, children without their coats, ignoring the mayor's proclamation, got up as ninjas and wizards, as disco queens and evil clowns and robots of cardboard and foil.

Hud drove into the pitch dark of Cherry Ave., the power still out in that part of town; even the streetlamps remained unlit. Then, just as a boy in a vampire's cape and widow's peak ran in front of the bus to egg its front window with a splat that made Hud's stomach jump, the houses along the row lit up all at once, their power restored. Plastic jack-o'-lanterns began to glow yellow, as did the eyes of an electric mummy on someone's front lawn. The cauldron of a witch on a roof flickered with purple and green, and from somewhere came the recorded bellowing of the undead. Hud had to park a moment and take it all in. Witnessing such a sudden return to life as usual lifted his spirit. He knew that what he was feeling was the next best thing to faith.